Klaudia Cay and the Witchfinder General

A.D.Hawkins

Published in 2016 by FeedARead.com Publishing – Arts Council funded

Copyright © A.D.Hawkins

The author or authors assert their moral right under the Copyright, Designs and Patents Act, 1988, to be identified as the author or authors of this work.

All Rights reserved. No part of this publication may be reproduced, copied, stored in a retrieval system, or transmitted, in any form or by any means, without the prior written consent of the copyright holder, nor be otherwise circulated in any form of binding or cover other than that in which it is published and without a similar condition being imposed on the subsequent purchaser.

A CIP catalogue record for this title is available from the British Library.

For Sarah as always.
To KK, Abbie and Millie.

To Anne with Best Wishes Christmas 2016

Contents

PART ONE
   Prologue
1. Time to travel — 1
2. A witches' brew — 9
3. How time travel works — 19
4. Witchfinders — 25
5. Called — 29
6. Gabriel Gubbins — 43
7. Mother Leech — 49
8. Earth. Fire. Water. — 59
9. Madeleine — 73
10. The road to Naseby — 79
11. Bury St. Edmunds — 87
12. The Green man — 99
13. Royalists — 107
14. Naseby — 119

PART TWO
15. Missing persons — 129
16. The Battle of Naseby — 139
17. Torture of the witches — 163
18. Bewitched — 177
19. Woburn Abbey — 185
20. Jac — 195
21. London — 199
22. The Grimoire — 213
23. Accused and condemned — 217
   Epilogue

PROLOGUE

Exod. 22.18.
Thou shalt not suffer a witch to live.

The sword rested easily in her hand. It felt natural. She had never fought anyone like this before. What could she do? The Roundhead did not know or care how old she was. That she was a girl, not a boy as she was dressed. She was the enemy. To be killed. He struck the first blow. She should have known it was coming, with everything Gabriel Gubbins had taught her. Where was Gubbins? Why was he not here, to fight alongside? She thought for a moment she saw him, running towards her from a wood. His brother, Nathaniel, was with him, but the image faded.

Too late. The searing pain in her side told her she had dwelled too long in this thought. Not fixed her eyes on her adversary's, to catch that flicker and sense where his first lunge would be. Now she was angry, at herself and at him, as she parried the next blow, found that split second between life and death. The sword in her hand had a life of its own, the thrust forward and upward slicing easily through the doublet. A crimson line in the white shirt, blood spilling as he staggered back.

His failed attempt at riposte met by her dervish spin, her scream as her sword sliced across his belly. Deep and fatal. His guts spilling into the hand that only moments before held the instrument of Klaudia Cay's death. Was she dying? Had his sword found her vital organs, now bleeding to her slow demise? The pain was intense, stabbing, deep in her stomach. She clutched at her side, saw her bloodied hand and cursed as the light was fading with her life force.

1
TIME TO TRAVEL

I woke up screaming. Mum was beside me on the bed.

'Make it go away, make it stop!' I screamed.

'You had a bad dream, Klaudia,' she said.

It's not the dream I say to myself. How can I tell her? All the things that happened. The Time Thing. Me with Gabriel Gubbins when I time travelled back to the 1640's. She would think it was the ravings of a disturbed teenage girl. Well, that's how they put it isn't it? Always going on about 'poor little Klaudia's problem'.

Well poor little Klaudia's not so little any more. It happened the other day in my history lesson. I thought I was going to die then and somehow last night it all got mixed together, just as I was going to sleep. Tummy cramps and then the scratching noises started again, behind the wall. It can't be I kept telling myself. I thought all that had finished after my last time trip, the one I hoped would really be the last. I just wanted to be, well, to be 'normal' or as normal as Klaudia Cay can be, with all her 'problems' and what we can't talk about: that I am a time traveller.

Mum got up from the bed saying how dirty and untidy my room was and that I needed to 'wake up my ideas' or something, and then she disappeared downstairs and not long afterwards there was a good smell of toast and coffee coming from the kitchen.

Yes, I drink coffee, we all do, me and my mates. You may remember them if you read my diary. Kat is my best mate; I hang out with her more than anyone now. We meet at McDee's and drink coffee at Costa. Simple. Except it's not that simple, my life. Neither is death. I know because I have come close, not just in the nightmare but on the battlefield in the English Civil War. I can tell you there was nothing civil about it. It was dirty and loud and bloody and lots of people died. I just wanted to forget my time trips but there is always something to remind you when bad things happen.

I lied. Well sort of lied, when I told you I never saw Gabriel Gubbins again. This was not true but how was I to know? No one told me what could happen in time. If you have read my diary you will know about Gubbins. He's a time traveller too. He was the bloke living in our farmhouse in 1643, when I made my first Time Trip. I miss him; we had some really scary adventures together.

I got dressed, went downstairs and had some toast. Mum said my room was minging. She shouldn't use words like that; she shouldn't use our language, if you know what I mean. I promised to tidy it up when I got back from school, and yes, I would muck out my pony tonight.

I was back at school, just like before, with Kat, Bran and Slick Alice. We were doing history and I kept thinking: what was it all for? I helped to save King Charles 1 and Oliver Cromwell from assassination by a Time Violator, but they still cut off the King's head. When you read about what they did to Cromwell's body after he died, well, was it all in vain? The battles? Gabriel's brother, Nathaniel, dying at the Battle of

Preston. The Lords Temporal sending me back three times to try and save history. Is that what we did? Me and Gubbins. Now I am in a mood. Our history teacher, Mr. Payne, picked me out and walked towards me.

"It would be a good thing for the rest of the class if you paid attention, Klaudia Cay, because they won't be happy when you are the cause of everyone being detained. Do you know the meaning of 'futile'? What Oliver Cromwell was trying to do was futile. The truth is he really wanted to save the King."

Well, he had a funny way of going about it, I was thinking. We had got to the bit about the Levellers in our history lesson. Mr. Payne was talking about the Battle of Naseby. I wanted to tell him that I was there in 1645 but of course I can't ever do that. Except with people who know about the Time Thing. The trouble is my old swimming coach, Shelley, who knew all about it, has gone to another school.

So it's only me, Kat, Bran and Slick Alice who can talk about it. Even then we don't say much, as if really it was only a dream. Maybe it never happened. More and more I keep thinking I imagined it all, travelling back in time, fighting Roundheads, our farmhouse in 1643 when I made my first trip and met Gabriel. But then there's Jac.

"Sir, why are we being punished because Klaudia Cay is stupid and can't pay attention?" Jac shouted from the back of the class. She is a nasty Goth minger and such a bully. Sadly, she's also the only other person I know, apart from Shelley, who has time travelled. It was Jac who nearly got me and Gubbins killed. Don't get me wrong, I have nothing against being Goth but Jac is the worst type of girl you could ever meet.

"I think we do have Klaudia's attention now, thank you Jac, and we don't need your interruption either." Mr. Payne turned around, walked back to his desk and picked up his book on the English Civil War. I stared back at Jac who had her tongue stuck out and made a rude finger sign at me. Then she looked as if she was going to shout something again but her mouth was stuck, her lips pursed. She was glaring at me as if it was my fault. She had a weird look, I could see she was trying to shout but nothing was coming out. She was starting to look scared. Good, I was thinking (I know that's mean) but what was happening? I knew that face, I had seen Jac really scared once, when I was using my 'Time Power' to send her and a Time Violator to Oblivion. She had begged me not to do it.

Mr Payne had started on again about The Levellers. As I ignored Jac and turned back I caught a glance from Kat. She had a funny look, and a bit of a cheeky smile, as if she knew something. She's very pretty, my mate Kat, and she can get people to bend over backwards if she wants something, like they can't resist her. My mum says Kat's a teen going on twenty-two. But I know that smile and it was telling me she was up to no good, I sensed some trick afoot. I gave her my 'I have a question for you' look.

My other mate, Slick Alice, has the desk between us and she saw what was going on with me and Kat. Then Kat passed a piece of paper to Alice and waved her to give it to me. Of course Alice looked at it and started to giggle. Now Kat is really good at art and she had drawn a picture of Jac with devil's ears, which was funny because it was Halloween soon and it looked so like a mask of Jac, with the ears.

Then I looked at what Kat had written underneath the picture:

'Mouth be closed, do not speak
No more trouble will you wreak
When sweeter words become your way
Then you can have your say.'

I looked again at the picture of Jac and realised the lips were sewn together. I turned back and Jac was staring at me across the classroom. She was furious but she couldn't say a word. I saw Kat give me a sign that said after school we would get together but we didn't for a few days because the pain started, as you will see.

Anyway, the Levellers. After the Battle of Naseby lots of New Model Army officers and soldiers, Roundheads or 'Parliamentarians' that is, started preaching sermons in churches. People did not like this but there was nothing they could do. The 'Upper Class' officers, who fought under the command of the Earl of Manchester, said these preachers were 'precious' men who had filled dung carts before they were officers. I laughed at this because I have to do 'poo picking' in the paddock where my pony grazes and some days I just hate doing it. I know there's a machine you can tow behind a quad bike which picks it up, much more fun, but my dad's too mean to buy one. I must have laughed out loud because Mr. Payne said:

"Klaudia, you seem to find it funny, do you have something to add on this?"

Well, I could tell him a thing or two but I bit my lip and said sorry, no. So these Levellers were rebelling against the army and causing everyone problems. One of the leaders, John Lilburne, was demanding religious liberty and 'manhood suffrage', whatever that is.

Cromwell said there was no other way to deal with the Levellers than to break them before they break you. I can understand that. I have to deal with Jac when she is bullying everyone as usual. Now I was paying attention because there was something about the Levellers I could not quite put my finger on, until Mr. Payne came to when King Charles the First was being 'confined' at Hampton Court Palace in 1647.

Cromwell was negotiating with the King but it was dragging on because the King was 'prevaricating' again about how the country could go forward. Cromwell got exasperated as well by the Levellers who were calling for dissolution of Parliament and demanding the leaders should pay more respect to the King's soldiers and their wishes. They produced a document, the Agreement of the People, which proposed that England should be a Republic. Now I was thinking about what happened when Gabriel Gubbins and I fought the Time Violator and lost a battle in 1647.

When I got home to my time England was a Republic and there was no Queen or Royal Family. I begged to go back and make things right. Well anyway, all this was going on with the Levellers and then suddenly it came together in my head.

What happens next is quite scary. Gubbins and I had saved the King's life and Cromwell's too in 1647, on November the tenth to be precise. What we did not know was that, some days before, Cromwell had sent a letter to his cousin Colonel Whalley who was guarding the King, saying there were 'rumours abroad of some intended attempt on His Majesty's person.'

The Colonel had shown the letter to the King who, it seemed, had also received a warning that certain Levellers had 'resolved for the good of the Kingdom' to take the King's life away. The following day, after we had saved him and Cromwell from assassination by the Time Violator, King Charles 1 disappeared from Hampton Court.

Just at this point in the lesson the pains started. It got so bad the teachers had to call my mum to come and collect me from school. As I was leaving Kat said it would be alright. She knew what was happening. So did Slick Alice. The becoming a woman thing. When I got home I felt a bit angry because they had never talked about it. How it was for them. Then I was thinking well, OK, don't ask me why but people don't talk about it, do they?

Then, just when I thought nothing else bad in my life could happen I had the biggest shock ever. I got a text on my mob. It just said: 'TIME TO TRAVEL'. Not who it was from or anything else.

Now this had to be Kat or Bran or Slick Alice, playing a joke, I thought, unless of course it was Jac. Before, when I time travelled, I had been 'Called' by Gabriel Gubbins and I had to have a 'Patron' who was Shelley, my old swimming coach. Could it be Shelley, I wondered? Those were the only people who knew I was a Time Princess. Or so I thought.

2
A WITCH'S BREW

I used to think history was pretty boring but that was before I started time travelling. Then it all began to take on a different meaning because I had seen things with my own eyes we were studying at school. Not that it's the only thing in my life. I also used to think dressage riding was namby-pamby. You know, all that fancy stuff on the horse in an arena, sometimes to music.

Everyone said it was the hardest thing to get right. Well, not for me, because I wasn't ever going to do it. All I wanted to do was cross-country and show jumping. But then three things happened. One, I realised that I wanted to do three-day eventing and that meant I had to do dressage. Two, I got a new trainer. They call her Scary Mary. I'll tell you more about her later. The third was I got a place on the national team and everyone said that is such an honour, to wave the flag and ride for your country. I hadn't been doing dressage long but it was much more fun and really intense than I thought.

Of course, not all this happened at once. I will try to tell you it all as it was. If everything went according to plan I would be on the team and go to Ireland, to Blarney where the famous castle is, and we would all travel in convoy. Mum and Dad would take me and they decided it would be great to stay on after the competition and we could all have a holiday touring around Ireland. I say all because my mate Kat was trying for the team as well and she was going to come with us on the tour. Cool! Me and Kat on holiday together. Now that was going to be fun!

Sorry, as usual I am getting ahead of myself. I still have to work through it to get on the team, and I have to win. You should know more about what's happened in my life since my last time adventure. Well, one thing that's important is that I am now older and wiser.

Up until now I had not really been doing very well in school. It had really started quite a long time ago but no one had worked out something was wrong with me. Just that I was different.

Well, it's true, I am different, not everyone is a Time Princess and only a very few people I have met are time travellers. But that was not the problem. I always had trouble reading and writing because all the words would get jumbled.

So they said I was thick, stupid, lazy, good for nothing. Of course, that made me angry and so much so I wanted to prove them wrong and when I found I was good at swimming, running, riding and shooting I had a chance and became a tetrathlon champion. A good job too because I had to use all my skills to fight the Time Violator, when I went back to the English Civil War. But that's another story.

The thing is, what I started to discover was if you were good at something at school there were other kids who didn't like it. And if you weren't good at something others would just make fun of you and start pushing you around. I had found that with Jac, when she was the new girl in my class last term. She's a time traveller too and it took all of my strength to fight back when we had our own battle in 1645.

It's like when Kat and I started to have sword fencing lessons. We go together and it's really good fun. Of course I do have an advantage because Gubbins taught me fencing so I could defend myself. Kat's pretty good too. When we both started winning fencing competitions Jac turned up with her mates and started jeering and causing a big disruption.

What changed a lot for me was when I started having dressage lessons with my riding trainer, Scary Mary. Everyone called her that (not to her face of course) because she was so LOUD and shouted at you a lot, and called you 'a worthless pile of unmentionable drivel' or worse (there are much worse things you can be called as I discovered).

Looking back I suppose I was pretty useless and everyone kept telling me how good Mary was for me because she stood no nonsense. Up until then I did not have a lot of respect for teachers, or my mum, least of all my brother and sister – that's what everyone tells me.

Now you should know Scary Mary was quite famous really as she was an international rider and had been in the Olympics and won a medal. Here she was, teaching little me – well not so little now. They were right, she shouted a lot but that's her way I discovered, and when you get it right she's full of praise and makes lessons fun.

One thing about dressage is you have letters around the arena and when you do a test you ride with different movements from one letter to the next.

Well, you can imagine straightaway I had a problem because I would get the letters mixed up and there would be lots of shouting and I would go into a mood.

Then one day Mary tried an experiment. I can't remember exactly what she did but there was lots of discussion going on with mum.

They called me over and asked me some questions I thought were really stupid and there was more hushed discussion with my mum, dad and someone else I did not recognise who had come to watch the training. Now what I did not know at the time was that, apart from my reading and writing, I was not good at paying attention.

Well, OK I was really bad at paying attention and when I got told off I couldn't handle it and would have a fit and shout at them and call them the worst names. It had become so bad they were talking about sending me to a special school where they would 'sort me out'.

It was Scary Mary who stepped in and changed everything. I wasn't supposed to hear the conversation one day but I caught what they said: that I was not only dyslexic but also seriously ADHD. That stands for Attention Deficit Hyperactivity Disorder. Now that didn't mean anything to me until they put me on medication, pills that is.

Now you can imagine how that made me feel; not good in the slightest. I found it made me quite angry and that is the problem. I get angry and frustrated and that makes it worse.

Anyway, they said at least they knew what was the matter with me, and that they should have found out years before but never mind, the pills would sort it. But Mary said it's not as simple as that. It would take a lot more, using all the energy in a positive way and that is when I won my first top dressage test. In fact it was so good they said if I kept it up I could get selected for the national team. Only a few more days to go and it's half term and next week is Halloween. Went shopping with Mum to get pumpkins – not for me you understand, it's for my little sister really, she's still a baby so she'll want to be trick or treating and do the whole dressing up thing. Dad says it's a good excuse to have some friends around at the weekend and that I can have my mates over so I invited Kat of course, and Bran and Slick Alice. Fun to all get together and I could talk to Kat about what happened to Jac the other day in school.

Alright, so we had some fun with make-up and got to look like scary ghouls and undead zombies. If you didn't know I live in an old farmhouse which is quite big and we have a long Tapestry Room with a big, open fire. It's my favourite place in the whole house because it has a secret passage that goes to a chapel next door.

Mum was getting things together for the party, dad was making mulled wine. George, my little brother, was being a prat as usual and had some of his mates from school over as well. There's not one I would want to go out with, they are all so ugly and think they are clever. Me and my mates would show them they are not. How? We'll think of something.

I had helped mum with making the food. Well you have to sometimes don't you? Where we had made the pumpkins into eerie lights with eyes and grinning mouths we had kept the pumpkin flesh. I peeled lots and lots of onions. That made me cry. We cooked the onions and the pumpkin with Italian sausages in the oven and I made a salsa with hot chilli flakes, tomatoes and garlic. "You girls can take yours up to the Tapestry Room." Mum said when everything was ready. We were allowed some mulled wine too! (Mum doesn't know I drink beer with my Granddad). So we sat by the big open fire. The food was good. The hot wine was really good. Best of all we had left George and his mates downstairs and only a few people, some Draculas and a couple of grown-up witches, sat at the other end of the room while they had their supper, then they went back downstairs and we were on our own.

"Come on Kat," I said, "was it really you in class who made Jac shut up? How did you do that? And what is this?" I had kept the piece of paper with the drawing of Jac and the rhyme.

"I made a spell, a stitched lips spell." She replied. It's a simple one really. I had to stop Jac talking about you, she's been bad mouthing you for days. I made the spell yesterday but it lasted."

"How do you make a spell?" Asked Bran

"How do you know about this Kat, you never told us?" Slick Alice looked at Kat as if she was seeing her for the first time.

"I have been learning about Wicca and I had some stuff in my room and my mum found it. I thought I was in big trouble but that's when I found out my mum is a witch."

"You mean a real witch, like the ones in Macbeth?" Bran had a bit of a clever look on her face, like she was mocking Kat.

"Be careful Bran," warned Slick Alice, "she might turn you into a toad."

"It's not like that. There are witches everywhere but you wouldn't know unless you have the special sense."

"And you have I suppose?" Bran said sarcastically.

"A bit, I only discovered it a little while ago, but it does work. You saw what happened with Jac." Kat reached into the satchel she had brought with her and pulled out a leather-bound book. It had a strange gold design on the front, a pentangle, Kat told us, a magic symbol.

"I found this in a box of my mum's stuff. She had told me to look for a box of old photographs in my dad's study room. There was going to be a family reunion and she wanted to do an album to show everyone. Anyway, I found the book. Maybe she wanted me to find it, her way of telling me she is a witch. It's called a Grimoire and it is our family's book of magic and spells. I am only just learning what it can do. My mum says I have to be very careful because it can be used to call up angels, spirits and daemons."

"Are you serious?" Bran asked, "you expect us to believe you're really a witch?"

"I told you, I am learning and my mum showed me some things she can do. It was scary at first but you get used to it. Anyway, you believe Klaudia can time travel."

"OK. Suppose you are a witch, what did you do to Jac?"

Kat took a square piece of white cloth from the satchel, and a marker pen, some black thread, a sewing needle, a candle and matches. She told us to turn down the lights.

"I just drew Jac's face on the cloth and wrote her name underneath." Jac's face stared back at us, her lips sewn up with the thread. "Then I said the words. The next day, when we were in class and she was being a pain I just drew her face on the paper you have, Klaudia, and I wrote the words underneath and it really worked. She couldn't say another word. Of course it's worn off now, all spells do."

"That's right and now I'm going to make you sorry you ever did it." The voice came from the far end of the Tapestry Room. Jac was standing there with some of her mates. They had gate-crashed our party. What was weird was she was wearing the devil mask with ears like the ones in Kat's picture of her, but it was definitely Jac, I would know her anywhere, even in a mask.

"You know what they do with witches, they prick them and make them confess and then really bad things happen to them." Jac spat out the words. "Just like what will happen to you Klaudia, when you travel again. You're being Called, I know, your Lords Temporal want you to go back and try and save King Charles from execution. You won't of course, but you may as well take Kat with you, you can be tried as two witches together."

"I am not a witch, I'm a traveller, I can't do spells and stuff." I said.

"You could have fooled me. You sent my Caller to Oblivion in 1647. People thought you were a witch then."

I was watching what Kat was doing. She had taken a mirror out of her satchel, then a small bag done up at the neck with a piece of cord. She opened the bag and took out a coloured stone.

"Onyx." She whispered. Then she poured some powder on the mirror. "Mugwort should do the trick." She placed the picture of Jac face down on the Mugwort.

"What are you doing Kat?" I whispered.

"Banishing spell," she replied, "to keep Jac away."

You cannot see me
You cannot hear me
You do not want me
Now let me be

She chanted the words under her breath. Then she put the onyx on top of the picture where Jac's face was and said the words again. Jac spoke.

"If you think your magic will keep me away then you've got another think coming."

But at that moment Jac disappeared. The trouble was, so did Kat.

3
HOW TIME TRAVEL WORKS

What I should explain to you is how the Time Thing works. At least as much as I know. When I travelled back to 1643 I had been 'Called.' That was the time I discovered I am a Time Princess. Now I know that sounds rather grand but it's really very scary because I don't know what's going to happen next. There are some people who are psychic and others are witches and then there are people who can time travel. Some of them are witches too but I never knew that Kat was one.

Well, I thought she must have travelled the way she disappeared at the same time as Jac. The thing is there are forces in the universe we can't really explain but the time travelling is something to do with Silicon, which is as old as time itself. It's no coincidence it's used in computers.

That's how I travelled the first time. But you have to have someone call you from the past (I haven't tried the future yet) and there has to be a good cause or reason to do so). Then there are the Lords Temporal. They look after Time. At least they try but there are also Time Masters and they are nasty and send people through time as well. People like Jac and her Caller, the Time Violator. Think about times you have been late, or a bus doesn't come on time or maybe something you are expecting in the mail doesn't arrive when it should. It's people meddling with time that cause these things, to upset the balance.

Before anyone can travel from my time, the present, to the past they have to have a Patron and mine was Shelley, my old swimming coach. The creepy thing is none of us knows who Jac's Patron is, it could be anyone, even somebody we know but we have no way of finding out. Shelley told me that once in every few hundred years a descendent of an ancient royal family of time travellers is born.

Lucky old me, I happen to be one of them. A big part of me wishes I was not, as I have already told you, but there's nothing I can do about it. Shelley said that it is the way of the Lords Temporal that they want to make sure there is someone who can fight on their behalf and send any Time Violators to Oblivion. That's a place in time where they keep travellers who have gone a bit crazy with their Time Power or those sent by a Master to change the future to their advantage. What to do about Kat? Where had she gone?

"Klaudia, where's Kat gone? Is she with Jac? What should we do?" Slick Alice was tugging at my sleeve. "If she's with Jac she could be in big trouble." Bran looked at me with an expression of worry all over her face.

"Shelley." I said, "I must call Shelley, she'll know what to do."

"But Shelley left the school Klaudia, we don't know where she is." Alice chipped in.

"I have her number, we'll call her." I started to look for Shelley's name on my mob when that message came up again: TIME TO TRAVEL. Now that gave me a shock. I tried Shelley's number. She had told me it was for emergencies only. Well, this was an emergency. I held my breath, hoping beyond hope she would answer.

"Klaudia, what's wrong?" Shelley had answered the 'phone.

"It's Kat, she did a spell and she disappeared with Jac. I think they must have travelled." I said.

There was a long pause, as if Shelley was talking to someone else, perhaps the Lords Temporal.

"They have." Shelly returned, "but there's nothing you can do, you have been Called again by Gubbins because King Charles I has disappeared from Hampton Court in 1647. You have to go there and find the King, or history may be turned again."

"Are Kat and Jac there then?"

"No, they are in 1645."

"Then you must Patron me and I will find them."

"No, your duty is to Gubbins and finding the King before the Levellers do."

"I don't care," I shouted down the 'phone, "I must save Kat, and you must send me."

"I can't, even if I wanted to Klaudia. I am no longer your Patron, you have a new one." Shelley sounded tired and resigned. At this point I must have started throwing a fit because Bran and Slick Alice got hold of me. I was shaking. Alice took the phone from me.

"Miss, it's Alice Penfold, what should we do, Klaudia is having one of her fits?"

"Put her back on the 'phone." Came the reply. Alice handed back my mob.

"Klaudia, now you listen to me. I can't help you but there's someone at your party who can. Find Mary and tell her what's happened."

"You mean Mary my riding trainer?"

"Yes, she's one of your new Patrons."

"And when did that happen?" I was fuming.

"Mary has been watching you while you're dressage training, she has to report to the Lords, to see if you're ready to travel again."

"You said one of my Patrons. Are there more?"

"There is another who will be revealed when the time is right." Shelley said firmly. I knew she would not tell me any more until she was ready so I thanked her and went looking for Scary Mary. I left Bran and Slick Alice in the Tapestry Room. Wouldn't you know it? Mary was talking to my mum and dad. I picked up a tray of glasses of mulled wine and went over to them.

"I think we need some more wine dad," I said, "these are the last glasses." Mary took one and smiled at me. Dad went off to sort the wine and mum said she had better see to some more food as well. Mary took me to one side.

"You're not quite ready to travel again Klaudia." She said. "The Lords Temporal want to see you better trained than last time. You still don't know how to use all your power."

"So it's true, you one of my new Patrons." I was probably wearing one of my cod looks at this point. "And who is the other new one?"

"That I cannot tell you until the Lords allow it." I thought we would leave it there for the moment.

"Do you know where Kat and Jac are?" I asked.

"In 1645." Mary replied.

"Then we must get them back."

"It's not that simple."

"What do you mean? I could go and bring them back."

"You are supposed to go to Gubbins in 1647 to help him find the King."

"So everyone keeps telling me. Mary, Kat's on the British dressage team and now she's missing. What are people going to say?"

"People disappear, Klaudia, it happens. They become missing persons. I have no power over Jac." I could not believe Mary was saying that.

"But Kat does have power with her spells and I do. I used my power before and nearly sent Jac to Oblivion with the Time Violator." I was about to throw another fit.

"I know, but I don't know what I can do..." Mary's voice trailed off. She closed her eyes as if she was hearing something in her head.

"I know, My Lord, but she is not ready." She muttered under her breath. "Then so be it." Mary looked at me squarely.

"The Lords Temporal granted you a special dispensation on your last trip Klaudia. They are prepared to do so again, to let you go after Kat and Jac if you promise to return and help Gubbins once you have found them and dealt with Jac. She has a Patron but we don't know who it is. You must find out so we can put a stop to her travelling again and meddling with time. Go to the chapel and be ready. Take Bran and Alice that far, no farther mind, and I will join you in a minute. There's something I must do first."

I went back to the Tapestry Room and, making sure no one else was around, pulled the candle holder on the wall. The door to the secret passage opened. Bran and Slick Alice followed me down the steps, bringing Kat's satchel and book with them. We used her matches to light a tallow torch left abandoned on a rickety table, and then we ran down the tunnel to the door at the end.

It was a tight space. There's a sliding wall that comes across when you reach that point but I knew about this and placed the torch in a holder next to the door. The door swung open. We moved quietly through the crypt and into the Chapel. Although it was dark there was a bright moon.

4
WITCHFINDERS

Two riders could be seen on the horizon. Their horses were walking at a steady pace and they were followed by a wagon, a rough cart drawn by a single Suffolk Punch. The big chestnut horse pulled the load easily, the burden being light with the cart driven by an old woman.

A makeshift canvas type of awning on a rough, rounded frame covered the wagon which contained a few provisions, some small wooden boxes and several sets of menacing-looking chains and manacles. There was also a strange chair mounted on a wheeled frame.

Anne Wright stood outside a humble thatched cottage by a pond and stream where she had been washing a skirt and laced bonnet. She stopped what she was doing and stared at the group arriving on the edge of the village. The younger man of the two riders seemed to be in charge. He looked to be about twenty-five or six and was dressed in a brown cape over a white, ruffled shirt, loose breeches, the colour of which matched the cape, and brown, knee high Cavalier boots with the bucket tops turned down. There were spurs on the heels.

He wore a capotain style hat, tall but wide as well at the brim, which gave an air of authority. Under this his hair was curly and long, reaching to his shoulders in the style of cut for 1645. He had a beard and moustache.

The other man looked older and dressed in a similar fashion though he wore no hat.

Anne had a sinking feeling in her stomach. So they had come at last and she knew it did not bode well for her, or for her friend who had emerged from the cottage to look at the arriving strangers. She was known as Mother Leech and she looked to the other woman as villagers began to gather around the riders and their wagon. Anne Leech, for her first name was Anne too, could barely conceal a fearful gaze upon the younger man who she knew to be loathed throughout the county of Suffolk. She knew only too well his name and what he stood for.

"Which of you is known as Mother Leech?" He asked.

"I be Anne Leech, and who, pray, are you sir?" Her pretence at not recognising him was convincing.

"Do you not know I am Matthew Hopkins, Witchfinder General? And you, mistress, should know your station?"

"I am your humble servant sir, as is my friend Mistress Wright. How can we be of service?"

"Two young girls appeared in this village I am told, as if from nowhere. They came not by carriage or horse, nor on foot. It has been reported to me from afar away as the County of Essex where we are about God's work, cleansing the world of those who commit not only acts of maleficium but who have pacts with the Devil himself. Are you these two young women?"

"Sire, we have lived here many a long year, as these good folk will bear witness, and you talk of witchcraft. There is not a man, woman or child who would accuse us of such an act. We just go about our business and attend church on Sunday." Anne Leech hoped no one would speak out against this.

"Then no others have passed this way, or appeared, as if from nowhere?" Hopkins questioned.

"None sir," she answered, "or the good vicar here would testify to it being so."

"Master Hopkins, we know of your good work in the County of Essex, word travels fast." John Lowes, the Vicar of Brandeston, spoke loudly so all the congregation could hear. "But a few weeks have passed since we heard of the trial at Chelmsford. Twenty three women were accused of witchcraft. Nineteen were convicted and hanged. The Earl of Warwick himself presided over the Justices of the Peace. If we knew of any witchcraft hereabouts we would be the first to inform the authorities and your good self."

"Then I trust, good vicar, that we have a bargain, should you hear of any in league with the Devil you will send word to me. I am officially commissioned by Parliament to uncover and prosecute witches. Indeed, I was responsible for extracting the truth from those at the Chelmsford trial. We will continue our travels to Yoxford where we have reports of a witch, Mary Clowes, and will return this way. Beware any who dare to defy Matthew Hopkins, Witchfinder General, and John Stearne, witch hunter."

He turned to look at the older man, then took off his hat and with a flourish waved the vicar aside as he firmly planted his horse in front of Anne Leech.

"Be afeared, Mother Leech, your name and presence in these parts have not gone unnoticed. We will return." At that, he and John Stearne led the wagon out of the village and onto the road for Yoxford. The villagers gradually dispersed, returning to their work and homes, leaving the vicar with the two young women.

"I know not how Hopkins came to hear of you as Mother Leech," he said, "we must take care who we talk to and look to God and the church for protection from this man. His own father was a clergyman, the Vicar of St. John's in Great Wenham and a popular man, more than can be said of Hopkins."

"Then how is it he became the afeared Witchfinder?" Anne Wright asked.

"It is said he overheard women in Manningtree discussing their meetings with the Devil. In truth, Hopkins began as John Stearne's assistant, though now he, Hopkins, wields the power. Be careful ladies, and I will pray for you." At this point the Vicar of Brandeston bowed and took his leave. The two Annes turned towards the cottage and entered the single room that served as both kitchen and living area. Before them stood two young girls, one visibly shaking with tears running down her cheeks. The other girl, the dark one, just smiled, a cruel looking smile.

"Where are we?" Asked Kat, brushing back her tears.

"You be in the village of Brandeston in 1645. We know what you are and how you travelled here. Worry not, you are safe now." Mother Leech reached for Kat to console her while Jac looked on and said:

"I wouldn't be too sure about that."

5
CALLED

We waited by the font in the chapel and I watched the water start rippling. Although the moon was very bright I turned on the lights. We were far enough away from home for anyone to notice. On my first time trip I was drawn through the screen on my computer but the other trips had worked around the chapel font. I was wondering how Scary Mary knew it was the place to go if I was to follow Kat and Jac. Then I thought about my Caller. Before it had always been Gabriel Gubbins, but he was calling me to go to 1647. At least I thought he was. I knew I couldn't travel unless I was Called and had a Patron to send me. Now I had two Patrons, in fact three according to Mary, and no Caller.

"What does it feel like, Klaudia, when you travel?" Bran interrupted my thoughts.

"It's hard to explain." I replied. "Sometimes it's just a tingle, others it's like being pricked all over with something sharp. Another time it was like an electric shock, the sort you get when you touch the electric fence round the paddock where I keep my horse. Very short and sharp."

"Does it hurt?" Slick Alice asked me. As I was about to answer Mary appeared.

"There should be a text on your 'phone Klaudia. You are called." She said. With everything else going on I had not checked my mob. I pulled it out of my pocket and there, on the screen, were the words: "I call you, Klaudia. Gubbins."

"How can that be, Mary, is he calling me from 1647? I have to get to Kat in 1645."

"You forget, Gubbins is a time traveller as well, Klaudia. He doesn't have your powers but he must have shifted a point in time to call you." I was a bit confused by this because I remembered when I was in 1645 before, I was caught in a Time Slip and Gubbins had been shot at the Battle of Naseby.

But I didn't get a chance to ask Mary anything else. I had put my hand on the rim of the font and I felt the tingle and then a sudden, painful, shock all through my body. I dropped my mob. I tried to say "no, I can't do this," but it was too late, I was travelling again.

***

The cottage smelled of wood smoke from the open fire. A large cauldron hung over the burning timbers, supported by a hook and two heavy chains attached to rails above, which allowed it to slide back and forth. Mother Leech leaned over the pot and gave the contents a stir with a long-handled metal ladle.

"A rabbit potage if you would like some," she offered, "after your journey here." Kat stared at the cauldron and shook her head.

"Not at the moment," she said "but thank you. I just want to know what I am doing here." She was still shaking.

"You're here because you're a witch," Jac sneered, "and anyway, it's your own fault, you tried to put a spell on me."

"You are both here for a reason," said Anne Wright. Kat looked at the younger woman. She could not have been much older than herself really and it was strange how similar they were. Both she and Anne Wright had blond hair and smiling brown eyes. Anne smiled at Kat, who couldn't help thinking it was a little like looking in a mirror or, perhaps, as if she was seeing herself a few years from now, an older Kat.

"I'll have some rabbit." Said Jac. Mother Leech cast a look at the dark-haired girl and the hairs on the nape of her neck stood up. She was sensing an aura from Jac, a foreboding, but she kept her feelings to herself for now.

***

An old man with white hair was staring at me in disbelief. Then he made a sign of the cross as he realised his legs were giving way and he stepped backwards to the altar, using it to support himself. We were in a church, a chapel bigger than the one at home. Looking at the man and his clothing I knew I had travelled and it must be 1645. At least it had to be if I was to find Kat and Jac.

"From whence came you?" The man stuttered as he eyed me suspiciously.

"From another time." I answered honestly. He paused for quite a long moment.

"Then you be the one." He said at last. "There was a prophecy which foretold three travellers would pass this way to help defend against the evil and fight the good fight. The others are already here."

"What others? Travellers like me?" I hoped beyond hope I was in the right place and time.

"Two young women like yourself appeared from nowhere. As we speak they are with Mother Leech and Anne Wright, though no one else in the village knows of their arrival."

"Who are you, Sir?" I asked, remembering my manners.

"I am John Lowes, Vicar of Brandeston, and by what name go you?"

"I am Klaudia Cay."

"And what have you there?" The vicar was pointing to the book in my hand. Until that moment I had not realised but I was holding Kat's Grimoire. I sort of remembered Slick Alice pushing it into my hand.

"Just a diary." I said, thinking quickly and hoping he would not ask to see it. Good thing I had it, Kat might need it if Jac was here too. We may need a spell to get us home I was thinking, because I had no idea if it was Gubbins who had called me or whether, without him, there was a way to get back to our time.

"Is there someone called Gabriel Gubbins in your village?" I asked the vicar.

"I know of no one by that name." He replied.

"Did you call me, are you a Caller?"

"I know not of what you speak. It will be best if I take you to Mother Leech for she will know what is to be done. I am just a man of the cloth and I know little of what magik brings you here. These are dangerous times for witches."

"I am not a witch, I am a Traveller." I defended myself.

"Some witchcraft brought you here to fulfil the prophecy. Come, we will away to find your friends."

Friend and enemy, I was thinking. Jac must have had a Caller to bring Kat here. What reason could there be, other than Jac wanting revenge for putting her under a spell? Somehow Kat and I would get out of here, back to our time as fast as possible. Of course, what I didn't know was that Jac and her Caller had plans for us and a lot of other people. None of it was good.

The vicar walked over to a table near the altar and picked up a bible and a hat with a round brim, which he put on once we were outside the church. Now he looks like a proper clergyman, I thought, as if he were about to deliver a fire and brimstone sermon; But we just walked quickly to a thatched cottage on the edge of the village.

I noticed a stream nearby and there was quite a big pond, like we have at home. Smoke was coming out of the cottage chimney and a familiar smell caught on the breeze. I knew there was some kind of potage cooking and I started to feel hungry.

"I have another witch and her name is Klaudia." The vicar said to a girl who came out of the door. I was about to protest again that I was not a witch when Kat appeared and ran towards me, tears streaming down her face.

"Klaudia," she cried, "it is you. They said you would come." As she threw herself into my arms I realised she was wearing a dress a bit like the Puritans you see in pictures, and then I noticed I too was wearing a dress with a bodice top and big brown skirt.

"My book, you brought my book." She exclaimed.

"So you can put a spell on Jac." I laughed. Kat looked at me with a big frown on her forehead.

"What is it Kat." I asked.

"Jac's gone." She said.

"Gone where?"

"I don't know. One minute she was here, eating some stew and then she suddenly disappeared."

"'tis true," the girl said, "she has some power but we could not sense whether she be a witch or some daemon."

"She's like me, we're not witches, we're time travellers, she must have travelled again, but I don't know where. She could have gone home I suppose. Knowing Jac she's up to no good wherever she is."

"I want to go home." Kat said, "I don't know how I got here, I did not do a time spell or anything."

"No, Jac must have had a Caller and brought you with her. Her Time Master can make that happen. But I don't know why." At this point another girl, a bit older than the first, stepped out of the cottage.

"Mother Leech, this be Klaudia," said the vicar, "the prophecy is manifest. Three witches from another time came this day." He said. I was about to protest again but Mother Leech answered as she pointed at Kat.

"This one is a witch, though she knows little of her craft, but a witch she is. The other two? I cannot be sure. For certain they have the power to travel through time to here from some future place. That much I can sense. I think though, the other, the one called Jac, although disappeared, is not far from here."

What is Jac playing at? I wondered to myself. I knew it had to be bad.

"We must be cautious," the vicar said, "the Witchfinder knew of the arrival of two young women strangers to the village, though how I know not. He will return, be sure of that, and when he does he will be looking for signs of witches he can have condemned."

"This Witchfinder, what is his name." I asked.

"Matthew Hopkins." Said Mother Leech. I looked at Kat and she was shaking her head in disbelief. We both knew about the Witchfinder because we had done some history on witches being hunted down, and it was not nice, I can tell you. We had been learning about William Harvey who was the physician to King Charles I of England. He was involved in a witch trial in Lancaster in 1634. Then we learned about Matthew Hopkins and how he was responsible for the deaths of hundreds of women accused of witchcraft. I had a very bad feeling about this.

"Come inside, before people see you." Anne Wright beckoned to us. We all went inside with the vicar following us.

"It is said that Hopkins was called to answer questions about how he came to be a witchfinder," the vicar related, "they say he met with the Devil and cheated him of his Booke, wherein were written all the names of all the witches in England. His answer to this was if he had been too hard for the Devil and got his Booke then it was to his great commendation and no disgrace at all. I received a paper from a good friend at the Justices, wherein Hopkins had answered these questions."

It was weird. I remembered this in our history lesson. Hopkins wrote about the witch hunts. It was true. The vicar had a paper which he took from his pocket and unfolded.

"It says in March 1644 Hopkins was living in a town in Essex called Manningtree where there was a sect of witches. Seven or eight by all accounts. These witches met on Friday nights and held Sabbats every six weeks, close by Hopkins' house; and made solemn sacrifices to the devil. Hopkins says he overheard one witch speaking to her Imps. Bidding them go to another witch. Now there were some women, he says, who knew about the Devil's marks and this woman was apprehended and searched. Her name was Elizabeth Clarke, a woman of my age, eighty years and some days, who was missing a leg."

"We read about her in our history," Kat suddenly said, "she had some warts or moles or something."

"Whatever it was, 'twas enough for the women with Hopkins to say she had three teats about her, which honest women have not. He obtained a command from the Justice to keep her from sleep for two or three nights. This way they would expect to see her familiars." The vicar was looking through the paper.

"On the fourth night, a quarter of an hour before they came in to a room where there were ten people, she described these familiars and called them by their names. There was HOLT, a white kitling and JARMARA, who was like a fat Spaniel without any legs. She said he sucked blood from her body. Then came VINEGAR TOM who was like a long-legged Greyhound with a head like an Ox. His angels transformed him into a child of four years without a head.

SACK and SUGAR was like a black rabbit. NEWES was like a Polecat. These all vanished away in time and the witch then named other witches with marks and Imps, whose names were ELEMANZER, PYEWACKET, PECKIN the CROWN, GRIZZEL, GREEDIGUT and more.

These accused as witches were taken and hanged and so Hopkins claimed the experience and skill to hunt and find witches." The vicar folded the paper and placed it back in his pocket.

"I will take my leave and mark my words be careful of this Hopkins, for who knows how far his power may extend?" The vicar turned to go, then looked back at us all. "It is said Hopkins is self-appointed as Witchfinder General. He claims he has Parliament's sanction to carry out these deeds of witchhunting. I hear tell that it is not true and that Parliament is concerned by his actions in these parts. Beware though, his power has already seen many more who may be innocents hanging by the neck, accused of having familiars and Imps that suckle at their third nipple and other blemishes. If the prophecy be true you, who travelled from another time, will fight this evil."

The vicar clutched his bible to his heart and walked off slowly in the direction of the church. There was the strong smell of the potage coming from a cauldron over the fire. A bowl of the stew was on the table, half empty. Kat saw me looking at it.

"Jac was eating the stew and just vanished, Klaudia," she said.

"Her powers are getting stronger, she is able to move around in time." I answered, convinced that Jac was drawing strength from her Caller. Where was mine?

Where was Gubbins? If this really was 1645 what date was it? Before the Battle of Naseby? Because that is where Gubbins had been shot and wounded and I was in the Time Slip.

Somehow there had to be a connection but I could not see how. I found myself looking at Mother Leech. Now you would think she was too old to have a name like that but she was not much older than me, I felt sure. She just looked older. Then I was thinking she looked quite like me, dark and mysterious. What was strange was the way Anne Wright and Kat looked very similar as well. This was beginning to worry me.

"Are you hungry, would you like some rabbit, Klaudia?" Asked Mother Leech. Now I had to admit I didn't really like the idea of eating rabbit but I was feeling hungry and anyway, this was the sixteen-forties. I had eaten all sorts of things the last time I was here. I thanked Anne Leech as she ladled out some potage and I took the bowl she handed to me. She cut a piece of bread from a fresh loaf and that was really doughy and nice with the stew.

"What are we to do, Klaudia?" Kat asked.

"I don't know, Kat. I'm hoping Gubbins is looking for us and will show us the way back." I said between mouthfuls, "but he's not in the village. We're in Suffolk and he lives in Oxfordshire. We might have to find a way to get to him."

"You cannot leave here," Mother Leech said, "the prophecy is to be fulfilled."

"You cannot stop us leaving." I was feeling the angry part of me rising. "Anyway, what is this prophecy?" I asked. She sensed my anger and did not answer the question immediately.

"My meaning is you cannot travel, it would be too dangerous with the fighting and the military all about, to say nothing of these witchfinders. Hopkins knew of two young women appearing here. He thinks they are witches, indeed he was almost accusing us of being so."

"Then we can't stay either," I said, "what if he comes looking for us?"

"The prophecy," Anne Wright replied, "foretold that three travellers would come to defend the innocents against the witch hunter. You must be the three."

"Two. Jac is not one of us, she's an evil, interfering bully." I was getting angrier.

"It is strange the way you speak of her, she being from your own time." Anne Leech looked at me questioningly. I did not think it would really help to try and explain about Jac. Somehow we had to get a message to Gubbins, I was sure. Then I started to get a really bad feeling. It was not one of Kat's spells that had brought her here, it was Jac and her Time Master; and now I was thinking it was not revenge on Kat. Jac wanted *me* here in revenge for nearly sending her to Oblivion. The more I thought about this the more I thought it must be true. That's why she brought Kat to Suffolk, so far away from Oxford and Gubbins. Somehow he had got me to here. Then he must know where I am. I hope he does.

"What we shall do is find a way to get you to Bury St. Edmunds," Mother Leech suggested, "because there are authorities there who can give you letters of safe conduct, if you must find your friend in Oxford."

"It would be best because Gubbins knows people who can help to get word to the Parliament, about stopping witch trials I mean."

"Then perhaps in that way the prophecy can be fulfilled." Mother Leech seemed to look relieved there was something that could be done.

"It is late and soon to be dark. We will ask Vicar Lowes in the morning to help in this matter. He will have a way to get you to Bury. Then you can help our cause." Anne Wright was looking at me in a strange way." Now I knew about the Cause, the secret society that had Intelligencers carrying news to both sides in the English Civil War. But this must be a different 'cause' I was thinking.

"You're witches, aren't you?" I suddenly realised how she and Mother Leech knew so much. They had to be witches, or Travellers. Or could they be both?

"Let it not be said where others may hear." Was Anne Wright's reply, "or fear we may be hunted like the poor women of Chelmsford."

"What happened there?" I asked her.

"Nineteen women were convicted of witchcraft and hanged." It was then I remembered. Because of the English Civil War the trial was conducted by Justices of the Peace and it was Matthew Hopkins who had made the accusations.

I had finished the bowl of potage and in my head I was trying hard to reach Gubbins. I knew my Patrons, Scary Mary and Shelley talk to the Lords Temporal, that's how they knew Kat was in 1645. Why couldn't I talk to the Lords direct I wondered? When I time travelled before there was a time when, somehow, I could sense what Gubbins was doing and where he was. I knew there had to be a connection but I could not find it, only that I knew Gabriel was not close.

"It is best you stay here tonight, lest any in the village

become suspicious of where you came from." Mother Leech interrupted my thoughts. "On the 'morrow we will decide what is best to do." I noticed Kat was looking through her book, her Grimoire.

"What is it, Kat?" I asked her.

" I am looking for a time spell," she said, "to see if we can get back home, I am sure there are some in the book, here, you put the date on a piece of paper and burn it, while you say: hear the words...."

"Stop now, say no more, you do not have the skill for such a spell." Mother Leech took hold of the book and turned some pages, "those who brought you here are too powerful, they will not let you leave. Simple spells may work but this book and time itself are not to be meddled with."

6
GABRIEL GUBBINS

Gabriel Gubbins could not understand what had happened. As a time traveller he was Klaudia Cay's Caller and though his powers were limited compared to hers, she being a Time Princess, he was a messenger for the Lord's Temporal. From time immemorial the Lords had battled against the forces of evil, the Time Masters, whose powers seemed to be almost equal. They could send destructive entities through time to cause havoc and wreak terror.

Gubbins in this life was the son of Sir Marmaduke Gubbins, a Cavalier who had fought for King Charles I. He, Gabriel, had 'Called' Klaudia Cay before to fight a Time Violator. In 1645 he and Klaudia were together at the Battle of Naseby. It was at this battle that Sir Marmaduke changed sides from the Royalists to the Parliamentarians, the Roundheads.

The King had not paid the Gubbins family what he owed them and they decided to support Oliver Cromwell in the hope the Roundheads would bring peace to England. Except for Nathaniel, Gabriel's handsome brother, who was an 'Intelligencer' for the 'Cause', a go-between passing messages to and from Cavaliers and Roundheads.

At Naseby, on the fourteenth of June 1645, Gubbins was with The Forlorn Hope of Musketeers, the soldiers who fought on the front line at the battle. Few would survive. Klaudia had travelled back to that time to fight the Time Violator. She had found Gubbins and had sworn to join the Musketeers and fight alongside him. But Gubbins persuaded her to look for his brother, Nathaniel and so to find the Time Violator to stop his attempt at killing both the King and Cromwell. For that was why she was there.

Gubbins was one of the lucky ones. The musket ball had grazed his ribs, entered his body through his shoulder and exited his back. He had collapsed into a ditch, with others who were already dead, and he was bleeding from the wound, sinking into unconsciousness.

It was the chill of the night air that saved him as gradually the blood stopped flowing from the wound and congealed on his shoulder. At some time in the night his clothes were taken from his body and he lay nearly naked in the putrid smelling ditch.

He was found the next day by two Roundhead soldiers and taken to be a Royalist. He was held prisoner. It was only by the stealth of his brother that he escaped. Nathaniel found him in the dead of the next night in a hospital tent, breathing but still unconscious, oblivious to the world of carnage and decay of the battlefield on which he had so bravely fought.

Now it was November 1647 and King Charles I, fearing a plot by The Levellers to end his life, disappeared from Hampton Court where he was held under house arrest. Gubbins only a short time before had said what he thought was to be his last goodbye to Klaudia Cay, the time traveller from the future he had named 'Somerset'.

When he rode with her again, a few weeks earlier in 1647, she dressed as a boy. Between them they saved the King and Oliver Cromwell from assassination at

Hampton Court by the same Time Violator who had been at Naseby. Klaudia had used her powers as a Time Princess to send him to Oblivion. Now, with the King disappeared and his life again threatened, Gubbins was hearing the Voices telling him to 'Call' Klaudia back to help him find and save the King.

He was feeding Petronella, the pig they kept for breeding, when the voices began calling. He was back at the Manor Farm, the family's farmhouse which, hundreds of years later, would become Klaudia's family home. Gubbins walked at a steady pace back to the farmhouse and climbed the stairs to the Tapestry Room, to seat himself at an oak writing desk.

Gubbins took a quill pen and ink and wrote on a parchment the words: 'TIME TO TRAVEL'. Clutching the paper he walked the short distance to the nearby chapel. He floated the parchment in the font water which began to gently ripple. The ink discoloured the water and as the writing faded so the parchment seemed to slowly melt away until it disappeared. He expected Klaudia to appear as she had done before but the ripples stopped and then nothing. Where was she?

"What ails thee?" He was startled by his brother, Nathaniel, who had stepped quietly into the chapel. The handsome and dashing young man was dressed as a Cavalier. He took off his hat and mockingly gave a bow.

"And whose side are we on today, Nathaniel? You should not be seen near Oxford dressed as you are, now the Parliamentarians have control."

"I have word of the King's disappearance from Hampton Court. Members of the 'Cause' met yesterday eve. Colonel Whalley, who was charged with guarding the King, became concerned when he did not appear for supper. On November the 11th, in the afternoon, the King told his secretary he had a long letter to write before evensong. When six o'clock came Colonel Whalley was not too worried that the King did not appear. By supper though he went and knocked on the King's door. There was no answer. Whalley peeped through the keyhole. The key had been removed and the door locked. He forced his way in through another door but found the room empty. The King, it seemed, had left by a back stairway and along an underground passage to the River Thames, where he met John Ashburton, a groom of the King's bedchamber and Sir John Berkeley waiting with horses.

They crossed the river on a barge and rode, it is said, for the Hampshire coast. That much we know and that the King feared for his life if he remained at Hampton Court." Nathaniel gave Gubbins a questioning look.

"Indeed there was already the attempt on his life. You know well Somerset and I saved him but a few days before from the one sent through time itself. Perhaps he learned of this?"

"What is abroad is that he feared the Levellers." Replied Nathaniel.

"Aye, but the voices tell me there may be Travellers amongst them who would do away with the King." Gubbins leaned against the rim of the font and his fists tightened on the edge.

"I have called for Somerset again. She is the Time Princess nominated for the task, to help save the King's life. What ails me is she has not come and yet the Voices say she has travelled from her time." Gubbins stared into the font water. It was at that point the parchment began to appear again and floated to the surface. Gradually a message formed and it read:

'Gubbins, you Called me, where are you? I am in 1645 again. Help me. Was it you who Called? Help me. Somerset.'

"What will you do?" Nathaniel asked.

"I must go to her."

"You mean to travel back?"

"It is the only way. I sense she is in grave danger." Gabriel Gubbins firmly held the rim of the font and in an instant he was gone.

7
MOTHER LEECH

Mother Leech lingered on a page in Kat's Grimoire.

"How came you by this book?" She asked Kat.

"It has been in my family like forever." She replied. We were sitting around the fire in the cottage. I kept looking at Anne Leech and it was really worrying me we looked so alike, almost like twins. Kat and Anne Wright looked like sisters too. I broke another piece of bread off the loaf and dipped it into some potage and stuffed it into my mouth.

Some of the stew dribbled down my chin. I wiped it with the sleeve of the black Puritan dress I was wearing. It felt quite comfortable, the dress, not like some of the clothes I had worn on my last time trip. They were rough and had made me itch. Kat's dress was like mine, trimmed with black lace and with a white lace apron. We had white lace caps. I took mine off.

"This book is very old and very important," Anne Leech continued, "we must take great care of it lest it falls into the wrong hands"

"What is so important about it?" I asked. "I mean it's just a book of witches spells and rhymes Kat's mum wrote in it."

"It is much more than that. This book was started in medieval times when the witch hunts began in England and Scotland, long before the Witchfinder General started his quest. This book contains ways to make amulets and talismans, not just spells and charms. Some parts of it are taken from much older times. There are magical incantations from Mesopotamia that could summon angels, spirits and daemons."

I was wearing my 'cod' look. My mouth was opening and closing but I did not know what to say.

"This is my mother's book and I have to take it back home with me!" Kat grabbed hold of the book from Mother Leech.

"How do we get home? I want to go home now." She had a worried look.

"In good time," Anne Wright spoke quietly, "there is nothing to be done this night. Guard your Grimoire as if with your life for its importance cannot be measured and 'twill be much needed in the days ahead."

Night was falling and the two Annes left Kat clutching her book as they started to light candles. The light from the fire was casting wavering, eerie shadows on the white walls and I began to imagine creatures, imps, appearing from the pages of the book and I thought about what the vicar had said, about imps suckling at nipples and blemishes and things. That made me think about the mole I have, I will not tell you where, and all the scary things that happened to witches in history.

Here we were in a cottage in 1645, with two witches, (I was certain now they were witches), and in a village visited by Matthew Hopkins, the Witchfinder General. He had come looking for two young girls who had appeared as if from nowhere. How could he know about Kat and Jac? Then there was the prophecy of three 'witches' from another time. Now the candles were burning, lighting the room, and there was a strange smell, like incense, like the smell in church when the priest swings around that incense burner thing, what's it called? A thurible my dad called it or a censer, I couldn't remember because I was feeling sleepy and I saw Kat's eyes closing like she was drifting off to sleep. I tried to keep mine open but the harder I tried the more tired I felt and then the room was full of dancing shadows, devil shapes and horned creatures and a witches' coven dancing round a fire. Am I travelling? Are we going home? Was the last thing I remembered thinking.

***

John Lowes had seen many changes in his fifty years as Vicar of Brandeston. For him, his sympathies lay with King Charles 1 and Queen Henrietta and the Catholics. He was a follower of Archbishop Laud, the Archbishop of Canterbury who was trying to steer England back to being Catholic. John Lowes' church was Anglican and over the years his villagers, as did much of Suffolk, favoured more the Puritanical ways, without images and statues in the church.

The vicar was now eighty years old and no longer liked in the village because of his beliefs. More than this, he was friends with the two Annes, Anne Leech and Anne Wright, who had appeared only recently in the village. Not as they had said when questioned by the Witchfinder General, Matthew Hopkins. No one had spoken out against the Annes because it was rumoured they were witches and could cast evil spells on any who crossed their paths.

No one knew where the two Annes had come from, though there was also a rumour one was from Essex, Hopkins' county. John Lowes' church at Brandeston had a fine church tower built in 1430 but the chancel, the eastern part of the church where the altar was, and other parts of the church, were falling into ruin.

Early in the morning, the day after the arrival of Klaudia in his church, John Lowes stood motionless in front of the altar, listening to Anne Leech and Anne Wright who were insisting he should help them with their plan. Mother Leech thrust a packet into his hands.

"Hide this in your tabernacle for safe-keeping and guard it with your life, for there is nothing in the world so filled with danger at this time." The two Annes turned to leave.

"What, would you have me defy the law and risk all in the name of witchcraft?" The vicar bellowed after them.

"If you do not, John Lowes, you may perish and your church, indeed the whole village be razed to the ground. You are now the guardian and pray God we can complete our task before the return of Matthew Hopkins." Anne Leech glanced back to see the ancient figure of John Lowes, still motionless but visibly shaking before his altar and his God.

I woke with a start and my head was all muzzy and I felt I needed another night's sleep. But then I often feel like that. My mum says it's just because I am a teenager, with growing and hormones changing and stuff. As I opened my eyes I could see Kat was still asleep, clutching a cushion where her book, her Grimoire had been the night before. I leaped up. The fire had gone out and I found we were alone. I shook Kat hard.

"Kat, wake up, they're gone and so has your book."

"Leave me, I want to sleep." I shook her again.

"Listen to me, the book has gone. It's only us in the cottage." At this she sat up sharply, wiping the sleep from her eyes.

"No!" She groaned. "Where have they gone?"

"I don't know, let's go the church and find the vicar. He'll know what to do." I pulled her onto her feet.

"Something strange happened last night. The candles, the incense, I think it was meant to send us to sleep so they could steal the book." There, I had said what was in my mind, "and if we don't get it back we might never go home because I don't know what's happened to Gabriel Gubbins. He has not answered my call. Now I am really worried."

"What is it that worries you?" The voice came from the doorway. There was a young fellow standing there, good looking if you know what I mean, with dark curly hair and tanned skin like leather, a bit of a gypsy look. He wore a white shirt with a ruffled collar but it was open, as was the short, hip length jacket and his chest was bare. He had baggy petticoat-like breeches, hose with red and white horizontal stripes and bucket top boots. He had a sword at his side. Kat began to giggle.

"He looks like a pirate." She whispered.

"He probably is." I giggled back. I took my bold 'I'm Klaudia' stance.

"And who be you sir who listens in doorways to private conversations?"

"Ah, let me introduce myself. I be Tom Cobbold, brewer, innkeeper and sometimes smuggler."

It was bold to admit to two strangers that you were a smuggler but he had confidence and I immediately liked this fellow with his charm and smile."

"I came to find the two Annes," he said, "we have fine victuals delivered to the inn and I promised them a share for certain favours past."

"They're not here, they are gone and we don't know where." I replied.

"Then come with me to the inn and I will send word to find their whereabouts, I am sure they can not be far." Kat glanced at me and I nodded a yes. I did not have a bad feeling about Tom Cobbold. We followed him into the village along the main street and to the inn, the Crossed Swords, where he poured two tankards of ale for us.

"Are we allowed to drink this?" Kat whispered the question.

"It is 1645, we're allowed to do a lot of things, just drink it." I said as I took a sip of the best ale I have ever tasted. Tom Cobbold's eyes twinkled as he looked at us both.

"And who are you fine young ladies, you are not from these parts?"

"I am Klaudia and this is Kat and we are travellers from the south." I half-lied. He took our right hands in turn and kissed each one. I remember Gabriel Gubbins did that the first time I met him and then I went red in the face. This time I did not but something about Tom Cobbold reminded me of Gubbins.

While we were drinking the ale there was a good food smell filling the air and a little while later Tom Cobbold disappeared into the back, to return with two pewter dishes of food, which he presented to us. Kat was staring at the fish. I was too but I knew something about food in 1645.

"Trout," I said "but how is it cooked?" I had not seen trout done like this before.

"Try and see, it is a new recipe. The trout be washed and trimmed, stuffed with mace, parsley, savory and thyme all minced small and pushed into the trout's belly, covered in half a pint of sweet wine and a lump of butter. Then stewed a quarter of an hour. Then you mince the yelk of a hard egg and strew it on the trout with a scraping of sugar, and lay the herbs about it."

It was really good, even if it was breakfast time in our time. I think Tom Cobbold was excited about the dish and just wanted us to try it. I was looking around the inn. It was not as smelly as ones I had been to in Thame and Oxford when I was in this time before. I noticed a pair of crossed swords on the wall over the big fireplace. Just at that moment Mother Leech and Anne Wright walked into the inn.

"I see you have met Tom Cobbold." Anne Leech cast a glance in his direction.

"Where is my book?" Kat's voice had a degree of anger at the back of it.

"It be safe with the vicar, he will guard it for you. He is to arrange your safe passage to find your friend. When you return you can have back your book as soon as we know you can travel to your own time."

"It's not your book to do that with." I could feel the anger rising in me and as it was now over a day since I had had my last pill the whole ADHD thing was building up. I could not be held responsible for my actions.

"You dare not travel with the book, it is too dangerous. In the wrong hands it could bring untold pestilence and destruction. The book is the reason you have been brought here. It is not by chance you came with it, Klaudia, nor that Kat was brought here with the one called Jac. It was to lure you and the book to this time. There are those who wish to seize its power. They will not stop until they have the book and its secrets. Find your friend, let him call on Parliament to end the witch hunts. The vicar will take care of the book meanwhile."

"How are we to find Gubbins?" I asked her, as I had another sip of the ale. I had been trying to reach him in my head but still he had not come. Then I had a thought.

"What date is it?"

"It be the 9th day of June in the year of our Lord sixteen hundred and forty-five."

"Naseby." I said. "That's where Gubbins will be." 'The big battle,' I whispered to Kat. She nodded.

"We must get to Naseby. How far is it?"

"As much as four, perchance five days ride." Was Tom Cobbold's reply.

"We need horses."

"I have horses, good horses, fleet of foot who will carry you there. But you can not travel as you are dressed, you can not ride horses in skirts, and anything can befall you on the way, women on horses in war when horse thieves abound and deserters shoot people on sight. We will find you breeches to wear, hose and boots, shirts and doublets, and hats to hide your hair. You will be boys to all who look upon you." I could see Tom Cobbold was amused by this.

Now I had done this before, when I was with Gubbins I was dressed as a boy known as Somerset, so that it would not look strange as we rode together with pistols and swords.

"We will need swords and pistols for protection." I pointed out.

"This we can arrange, muskets too," Tom Cobbold smiled, "we have those aplenty."

"You will need money, to pay for food and to stop in inns along the way." Mother Leech suggested.

"Why are you helping us? You have taken my book. What do you want from us?" Kat asked her.

"Because we and all godly people in these parts are afeared of the Witchfinders and their power. Innocent people are being hanged as witches, though it takes a great many others, constables, justices, accusers and fearful folk to bring people to trial as witches. But it is Hopkins who makes the first accusations as if they come from God himself and brings them to confess their league with the Devil. If you can find your friend he can petition against the Witchfinders. Return with him and you will have your book. Together we will find a way home for you."

So in a few minutes, drinking ale and eating trout in an inn in 1645, it was decided that Kat and I would become boys and ride for Naseby.

8
EARTH. FIRE. WATER.

I was at Naseby before, in the battle, on one of my other time trips. It was where a Time Violator, who was trying to assassinate Oliver Cromwell and King Charles, had defeated me. I remember falling into a Time Slip where I was trapped and had no power to change events. I even saw Gabriel Gubbins shot.

Now I was thinking if we could get to Naseby before the battle started perhaps I could change the way it was, before Gubbins joined the Forlorn Hope of Musketeers and before I was defeated by the Time Violator. But life isn't that simple is it? I began thinking as well how I could be in two places at the same time. Now that was worrying. Anyway, if we could find Gubbins maybe there was a chance for us and all the people of Brandeston to be rid of the Witchfinder General. We only had five days.

I realised Tom Cobbold was looking at me in a, well, in a way, if you know what I mean.

"How old be you?" He asked.

"Sixteen." I lied.

"And you?" He looked at Kat

"The same." She said.

"Then you should not ride alone on this journey. I will come with you to see no harm befalls you."

"That's very kind," I said, "but it is not necessary, we can look after ourselves."

"No protest," he countered, "I am to ride with you. Where came you from, you are not of these parts, your accents are strange, where do you live?"

"At this moment with us." Anne Wright interrupted. You do not need to know from whence they came, indeed it would be better that you don't, with all the talk of witchcraft hereabouts. If you do not know, you can not speak of it." He seemed to accept this easily and no more was said on the matter.

"Come, we will away, there is work to be done while Master Cobbold and the vicar make arrangements." Anne Leech motioned us towards the door.

"The vicar?" I asked.

"You will travel with him to Bury St. Edmunds where he has influential people who will draw up papers to help you travel. The Royalists are coming nearer and the country is at war. It will not be safe for you without correct papers." Mother Leech was emphatic. We left the inn and returned to the cottage where she and Anne Wright lit the fire again and placed a different cauldron over it. They began to chant incantations as they dropped different things in the pot.

EARTH. FIRE. WATER.
All three
elements of Astral
we summon thee
Protect this day
Kat and Klaudia Cay
In no way shall this
spell reverse or
place upon them any curse
So mote it be

"So mote it be." Anne Wright echoed Mother Leech's words.

"So you are witches then. Is this black magic?" I faced Mother Leech.

"We are of the white witches' craft, not the Black Magik."

"What have you put in the pot?" Kat asked.

"Aqua above the fire, earth from under your finger nails which we cut and we took hair from your heads, all when you were sleeping."

"You drugged us didn't you?" I felt my anger rising again.

"A mild potion in the candles, only so you slept well enough for us to prepare to give you protection for what is about to come."

"And what is coming?"

"Apocalypse, more battles between the King and Parliament's army, death, pillaging, rape across the land. All these things the war has brought and more. The rise of the Witchfinder General, hunger, privation, and disease throughout England." It was true, what Mother Leech was saying. In just a few days the Battle of Naseby would see more than a thousand people dead or taken down by the guns of war, their bellies ripped open by pikes and swords, limbs severed and bodies maimed.

"And you can see all this?" It was as if I believed Mother Leech could see my images of Naseby with her witch's third eye. I think she could. Kat asked what else was in the brew in the cauldron but neither of the two Annes would give her an answer, saying she would learn all these things in good time. Good Time. That's what we needed on our side to reach Naseby, find

Gubbins and petition for the end to witch hunts. Nothing is easy.

Mother Leech took a small leather flask and placed it in the cauldron, collecting some of the potion. She handed me the flask.

"This potion is protection too. In times of trouble sprinkle a few drops around you, like holy water, and it will ward off daemons, evil spirits and incursors."

"Do we drink it as well?" Kat asked, almost mockingly. It did all seem a bit dramatic but then in 1645 people were afraid of these things and anything bad that happened to people and their villages, they had come to think, was because of evil, witchcraft and the Devil himself. I knew this from history and it was why Matthew Hopkins was, as he put it, in demand to hunt the nation's witches.

"You do not drink it. Cast some drops around to protect you, when you are sleeping in an inn or some barn along the route as you travel to Naseby." Anne Wright handed to Kat another small flask she had filled with the potion. There was a sound outside, a dog barked. In the distance we could hear the noise of wagons and riders coming, the horses' hooves echoing in the street through the village. Anne Wright stepped outside and quickly ran back in.

"'tis the Witchfinder. Go, run, find the vicar and Tom Cobbold at the inn. Get away from here before it is too late. We raced outside, only to see our route to the church was cut off by the advancing riders and carts. There was a small bridge over the river so we ran for this and crossed it, into a thicket where we could hide but still see the cottage. As the riders and wagons came into full view I could see the leader and I knew it must be Matthew Hopkins. I remembered when we were doing witch hunts in history we looked up Hopkins on the web. He wrote a book called: 'A Discovery of Witches' and there was a picture of him on the cover, with the beard, the tall hat, cape and bucket top boots. In the picture he looked quite old but this fellow was not that old, about the age of one of my cousins and he is twenty-six or seven.

With Hopkins was another man and following them were riders, who looked like soldiers in the Roundhead army, and then the carts. One was driven by an old hag and then I realised, I had to put my hand over my mouth to stop myself from shouting. There was a girl sat next to her and it was Jac from school. I did the hushed finger sign to Kat who was shaking her head in disbelief. Behind Jac and the hag, in the open wagon was a woman in manacles and chains, quietly sobbing.

Mother Leech and Anne Wright had come out of the cottage and were staring up at the men on horseback and my heart leapt for them. So Jac must have brought Kat here and somehow she was in league with the Witchfinder General. Somehow as well, they must have known I would follow or be sent. But what could they want with us? The book. Kat's Grimoire. Mother Leech had said how important it was. Perhaps that was it.

Then I had the thought that Hopkins was Jac's Caller, like Gubbins was mine. We could not hear what Hopkins was saying to Mother Leech but by the expression on her face it did not look good. Suddenly, two soldiers got down from their horses and grabbed Anne Leech and dragged her towards the pond near the cottage. Two more men pulled a strange chair out of one of the wagons. It had ropes attached to it. Then they got more ropes and they tied Anne Leech's hands to her toes, attaching the chair to her with the ropes.

I could not believe what they did next. They threw her into the pond, with a man either side holding the ropes attached to her and the chair. I was about to rush out and shout at them to stop. I could feel a fit coming on but something held me back. I was getting control of my ADHD and what it does to me, I was thinking but then I realised that Kat was holding onto my hand, squeezing it so tightly it hurt, stopping me from running across the bridge.

"What can we do, Klaudia, this is horrible?" She whispered. Mother Leech had sunk in the pond, upside down, only her skirt could be seen billowing on the surface. Then suddenly her head appeared and she was gasping for air. I could see what was happening. The two men were pulling on the ropes and she was being held up by the chair. What could all this mean? Now villagers were gathering to watch the spectacle, some shouting and jeering. The wind carried some louder voices and we heard them chant:

'Witch, witch, the witch she floats, the witch she renounced her baptism, she is a witch, and this one too.'

Some of the villagers had hold of Anne Wright who was trying to get away from them. The fellows with the ropes pulled Mother Leech across the pond to the side and onto the bank. She laid coughing and gasping for air as the men untied her ropes and put her in manacles.

Then they secured Anne Wright to the chair and did the same as they had done to Mother Leech, made her 'swim' by throwing her into the pond. I remembered now, it was called the 'swimming test'. If she sank she was supposed to be innocent, if she floated she was guilty of being a witch. I was so scared for her when she did not come to the surface, I was sure she was drowning.

But the men did the same trick, pulling on the ropes until she was floating and the villagers continued their 'witch' chant. Anne was choking and coughing and had a terrified look as they dragged her to the bank. She was put in manacles as well and the other woman was pulled out of the wagon, her chains unhitched. They and Mother Leech were pushed roughly into the cottage, followed by Jac, Hopkins and some of his men.

All this time Jac had been sitting on the wagon's buck board. It was the first time I had seen her smile or laugh, like she was enjoying the whole evil thing. I felt helpless. We had no pistols or swords, what could we do? I could only think we should do as the Anne's had said and try to get to the vicar and Tom Cobbold. Surely they could do something. The church was nearest so I whispered to Kat that was where we would go. Maybe if the vicar would give us back Kat's book she could do a spell or something to stop all this horror.

We had to cross the bridge and to do this we would be seen by the fellows still outside the cottage. Then, luckily, the other important-looking one came out of the cottage and spoke to them. They pointed to some of the villagers, picking them out, and together they all went through the front door. The rest of the small group of villagers seemed to melt away, back up the street.

"Come on Kat, this is our chance." I whispered. We crossed the bridge stealthily, keeping low by the stone wall until we came level with the cottage. I could not help it. I just had to look in. There was a window open and we peered into the room. I know it was dangerous but sometimes you just have to deal with it. The villagers who had been chosen were sitting like a jury at a trial. Matthew Hopkins was standing watching, as the old hag produced some sharp needles from a bag. The other men were holding the two Annes and the woman from the wagon. Hopkins turned to her first.

"Mary Clowes of Yoxford, you be accused of being a witch. Like these two here you failed the test to swim. How plead you?"

The old woman had tears streaming and she whimpered.

"I am no witch, just a poor woman whose husband is killed in the war. All I had left was my humble dwelling and my cats."

"Familiars!" Said Hopkins, emphatically. "Imps that suckle at a pap or teat about your person."

"You have no right to accuse me of such." The woman sobbed.

"I have command from the Justices to determine if you three accused are witches and this we will do by proven means and with these good villagers present. A matron, a midwife, a doctor and others will bear witness this night and for two or three nights more, if Imps be called and witchcraft practised in this place. Strip these women of their clothes and let the search begin. We look for the same marks as were found on other witches in our Hundred in Essex."

I did not believe it when Jac and the old hag started pulling off the womens' clothes. I did not want to watch any more. I pulled Kat away from the window and we set out for the church.

"That is so horrible, what they are doing." Kat was still holding my hand in a tight grip.

"That really is Jac isn't it? What is she doing Klaudia, why is she so nasty? We must stop her and get home."

"I know, Kat, but I think Hopkins is Jac's Caller. He brought her and you here, and I think he knew I would follow with your book. I'm sure that's what he's after. Don't ask me why. I think he must be a Traveller but I don't know why he is hunting witches, or people he thinks are witches." Nothing had prepared me for this. It was scary and I wished Gabriel Gubbins would come and help.

"We'll find the vicar and tell him. He will know what to do." I squeezed her hand and we began to run towards the church. I could see two figures in the churchyard. As we came closer I could see the vicar was talking to Tom Cobbold, the Pirate, as we liked to think of him. We approached and the vicar looked very concerned.

"You should not be seen, come inside, quickly." We went into the church with him and Tom. I started to tell them what Hopkins was doing to the poor women in the cottage but the vicar halted me.

"I know of what they do. They will use trick needles and prick parts of their bodies. 'Marks' they call them, perhaps a wart or something that might look like a third teat, in any part of their body, to see if it bleeds. If it does not, this be a sign of the witch. They are clever, for the needles they use do not pierce the flesh; they become concealed in the handle, making it look as if it has entered the body without letting blood.

"Then they keep the accused witch awake through the night, taking it in turns while the village folk observe. They expect in two or three nights of the witches not sleeping to see their familiars appear. It is believed that the Devil works with these familiars to find entrance to the body and use the organs of that body to speak with and make a pact with the witches."

"Can you not stop them, you are the vicar. There must be something you can do?" I could not believe the vicar and Tom Cobbold could just let this happen.

"It is beyond our power. Hopkins, the Witchfinder General attends only those cities, towns and villages who have called him to hunt down witches. He is paid by these said places such as Yoxford and now Brandeston. The village has invited him here. They have paid him because they fear Anne Leech and Anne Wright and others are witches and the cause of all ills that befall the village over time. Indeed, there are some who are accusing me, their vicar for fifty years, of being a witch too." I was in disbelief. For once I did not know what to say. Tom Cobbold came to my rescue.

"Come, follow me, we will away to the inn and prepare you for your journey. There is nothing to be done at this time for those being accused. This torture Hopkins uses could make the women confess to your presence. You have appeared as if from nowhere but I am not the one to question where you came from or what you may be. I will help you find your friend, this Gubbins, if he be the one to save the day."

"They might even force them to tell of the whereabouts of the book, Klaudia, the one you brought with you when you appeared here in the church." Said the vicar. "It's my book," Kat cut in, "where is it? I have to have it to take home, it belongs to my mother, for her spells."

"Ah, so it is a book of magik, the vicar looked at me

dubiously and I remembered I had told him it was my diary. "Then all the more reason for it to be kept safe with me until you return to Brandeston. The Annes wished you do not travel with it in fear it may fall into the hands of the Witchfinder General."

"Why is it so important, why would he want it? It's just a book of spells." I started to shout.

"Hush, it is not as simple. The book holds ancient scripts and is more than you could imagine."

"Then tell us, tell us what is so important." I was getting more and more angry. It was obvious the vicar knew more about the book than we thought.

"Part of the book is of this time, from King James 1 until now, parts written earlier, others later. The book holds a secret, or secrets and the Annes believe it is what Hopkins wants, the secrets therein. I know no more than this. Now you must go with Tom and prepare for your journey. I will accompany you to Bury St Edmunds, where there is a bishop I know who will provide papers for safe passage if you are challenged by Royalists; and there is a Justice who can do the same should you meet Parliament's men. Here are two letters of introduction, lest for any reason I be detained before you reach Bury."

"Where is the book?" Kat began again but there was a banging on the church door and we could see Hopkins' men through the window. Before we could do anything Tom Cobbold had pushed us to the back of the chancel. He touched the hand of a statue of the Virgin Mary, one of only a few statues in the church. The statue turned and a door in the wall opened.

"A smuggler's secret route." Tom smiled at me. We ran into a passage and the door closed behind us. It was like being at home where we have the secret passage which was a 'Priest's Hole' where they would hide Catholics in the time of the Guy Fawkes and the Gunpowder Plot. Where this passage led I could not guess. We didn't seem to be anywhere near the sea. We kept running as if our lives depended on it. Which they probably did.

***

To Gabriel Gubbins the surroundings were familiar, as if he had been here before. He sensed he was in the right time, in 1645, and that Klaudia Cay was in this time as well. But somehow he also knew she was a long way away. His attempt at finding her had been thwarted by his arrival in another part of the country. Some power had deflected his progress through time. It was a sense of déjà vu that surrounded him. His father, Sir Marmaduke Gubbins, had changed his allegiance from King Charles 1 to support for Oliver Cromwell and the Parliamentarian army. Gabriel was unsure whose side he was really on but for now he would be with the Roundheads. What he did know was that he was on the outskirts of Oxford, not far from his home, with General Fairfax, Commander of the New Model Army in the besieging of the city, the King's headquarters.

Much of the King's army had gone north with Prince Rupert of the Rhine, to join forces with Scottish Royalists and recover the North of England. Oxford was becoming short of provisions and the Royalists could not hold out much longer. To distract the Roundheads, the Royalists stormed the Roundhead garrison at Leicester and Prince Rupert marched south to relieve

Oxford. General Fairfax was ordered to abandon the siege on Oxford and move north on the 5th of June. Gabriel Gubbins was amongst those sent to engage the King's army and he found himself on the road, marching to an uncertain fate.

9
MADELEINE

"Halt!" Tom Cobbold commanded, as if we were in some military operation. We had reached the end of the secret passage from the church and now we stood in a small underground room with just one torch burning, casting both light and shadows on the walls. There were stone steps leading up to an oak door.

"I will make certain we are safe." Cobbold climbed the steps, his sword in his hand. He slowly eased back the door and a flood of daylight filled the room. He disappeared through the doorway for a moment and Kat and I heard voices. Then he returned.

"It is safe, come, we are at the inn." We leaped up the steps, glad to be out of what was a dark and smelly room. A very pretty girl stood before us. She was about our age, perhaps a bit older. Her features and hair were dark, Spanish-looking, like Cobbold. She had high cheek bones and dark brown eyes. She smiled at us and I knew we were going to be friends.

"My sister, Madeleine, she looks after the inn while our father is away at the war." Tom Cobbold introduced us. What about their mother? I wondered. He seemed to sense what I was thinking because he said: "our mother passed, less than a year ago. She was held in gaol, accused by Hopkins of being a witch. She was released by the magistrates, for there was no proof against her, but the Lord took her soul. She died of consumption." I was sad at this but Madeleine interrupted and said, "come, we must prepare you for your journey, away from Brandeston and Hopkins, before he learns of your presence here." She showed us upstairs to a room, made dark by the Jacobean oak panelling on the walls but lightened in some parts by bright woven tapestries. It reminded me again of home.

Madeleine pulled a handle on one of the panels and it revealed a wardrobe behind the door, full of men's' clothing and boots. She reached in and pulled out blue breeches and white shirts, hose and blue jackets with silver buttons down the front, leather waistcoats for protection from sword strikes and finally some really nice long leather boots with the tops turned down. I noticed they had broad toes. Cavalier boots, I remembered, because the toes were broad. Puritan boots had pointed toes.

"Try these for size." Madeleine held up two pairs of breeches and two shirts. I noticed she had an unusual accent which I could not place. It sounded foreign, with a lilt. We slipped out of our Puritan dresses and put on the men's' clothes which, surprisingly, were not a bad fit. It was then I realised they must have belonged to Tom. I was not sure how I felt about putting on his clothes but I was certain we had no choice if we were to travel to Naseby without drawing too much attention. Tom Cobbold had already said he would travel with us, as if we were brothers together, bringing news to our father that our mother had died. Well, it was a story he made up in case we were challenged.

There was no mirror in the room so I couldn't really see what I looked like but I looked at Kat and she looked at me. We agreed, we made pretty good boys, especially when we put on the hats with the feathers.

The boots came up to our thighs, with the tops turned down, but they were comfortable and I knew we could ride in them. While we were trying on the clothes I swear there was a moment, a millisecond, when Madeleine disappeared, then reappeared, ghost-like.

I thought I must be seeing things. We went downstairs and Tom Cobbold had a smile on his face.

"You look like fine young Musketeers. We must arm you as such." He had in his hands a pair of swords and scabbards with leather belts. He handed us these as well as two flintlock pistols, both loaded, I could tell. There was a smell of gunpowder. I noticed he was now armed with two pistols in his belt as well as his sword. He was dressed like us and I thought it was funny. We were like the Three Musketeers, Athos, Porthos and Aramis. I sort of wanted to be d'artagnan but he wasn't one of the three. Before Tom Cobbold could say any more, three men walked into the inn. I knew instantly they were Hopkins' men.

"Who will serve us here? We have a busy day and night ahead, dealing with witches. You wench, ale for me and my men." The man directed the command to Madeleine who quickly poured three tankards of ale. I realised the man giving the orders was Matthew Hopkins.

"Have you seen two young women, strangers to these parts?" He asked Madeleine.

"No sir, no strangers have been seen in the village, apart sir from yourselves."

"And you know who I am?"

"Yes sir, you be the Witchfinder General, asked by the village to find witches therein."

Until now, Hopkins appeared not to have noticed

Kat and me but now he turned in our direction.

"And these young fellows, where are you from?" Now Hopkins was eying us suspiciously and I realised it was probably because we were wearing Royalist musketeer colours.

"They are my brothers sir, come from Manningtree, where I used to live." Tom Cobbold spoke for us.

"They bring news of our mother's death, news we are to convey to our father who fights in the army."

"Your name sir?"

"Tom Cobbold." Hopkins' expression changed for a moment, as if there was some recognition of the name, but then he appeared to dismiss the thought.

"In which army does your father fight the war?" He asked, in a Puritan way I thought, as if he was judging us.

"He fights for justice, peace and the good Lord." Tom deflected the question, which Hopkins seemed to accept because he turned back to the tankard of ale and started drinking. We slipped quietly out of the room, relieved we had been accepted as Tom's brothers and not accused of being Royalist. Tom led us back upstairs to a bedroom with a view into the main street below.

"You can wait here while I assemble horses and muskets. I will go now." Tom Cobbold took two money bags from his pocket and handed them to us.

"From the two Annes and me, silver coinage for the journey." He turned and left the room. We threw the pistols and swords onto the bed.

"Klaudia, is this really happening? I want to go home, I'm scared. Can't you do something?" Kat pleaded.

"I'm just hoping we can find Gubbins and the way

back. I don't know what else to do. Hopkins has the two Annes and that poor woman and probably the vicar too. We were lucky the Witchfinder didn't realise who we were, girls, not boys."

"So we can't get to my book. What about the secret passage back to the church, we could go that way."

"And where do we look for it? The vicar did not say where it was hidden, only that it was safe. Don't you know any spells to get us out of here?"

"Not without the book. Even then I don't know if they would work. I have never tried before. Mother Leech said time travelling spells are very difficult but I know the book has special powers. I feel it when I hold it, as if it is talking to me, helping me to understand the ways of old, when witches and seers, soothsayers and oracles were respected and consulted. Not like now when they are hunted and hanged." Kat was getting really upset and I felt one of my fits coming on.

"Look. We could go to this Matthew Hopkins and tell him who we are and that if he releases the Annes and the vicar, if he has him, and lets them help us go home, he can have the book." A look of horror came over Kat's face.

"He must not have the book, Klaudia, it is calling to me, telling me there are secrets that must not be learned by the Witchfinder. Secrets that could make him so powerful no one knows what might happen for the rest of time." Those last words remained with me. 'For the rest of time.' As I stared out of the window, Hopkins and the two soldiers were leaving the inn, walking down the street when they stopped and turned. The Witchfinder was pointing back at the inn. The two men started to walk back as Hopkins continued down the street towards the witches' cottage.

A few moments later we heard screams from downstairs. It was Madeleine. Without thinking we ran down and into the bar. The two men had hold of her and were dragging her to the door. I reached a hand instinctively for a sword but there was none at my side.
We had left them in the room along with the pistols. I had a fit. I jumped onto the table near the big fireplace and grabbed the crossed swords off the wall, tossing one to Kat who caught it and started to brandish it in her hand. The two soldiers were so surprised it took them a moment to realise what was happening. They released their grip on Madeleine and went for their swords. But we were faster, although the sword was much heavier than I was used to. This was why we were here, in 1645, to fight for justice. Now the men had rallied. They drew their swords and they came for us.

10
THE ROADS TO NASEBY

The New Model Army musketeers looked resplendent in their red and yellow uniforms, even though they had been camped for the besieging of Oxford. Orders had come and the army began the march north to confront King Charles 1 and the Royalists. Gabriel Gubbins had fallen in with the foot soldiers. Usually he would have been astride his horse but horses had been commandeered for officers. At this point in the war, horses were becoming in short supply.

Three day's march saw the advancing Parliamentarians nearing Daventry, where they rested awhile and made camp for the night. Both the Roundhead and Royalist armies had women camps following them, camp whores many would call them. In truth there were women whose menfolk were in the army, and other women who cooked for the soldiers, as well as those who would do certain favours in exchange for money. Many came from Ireland and large numbers from Wales. This advancement was no exception and the women made camp close to the soldiers' encampment.

As evening drew on the cooking fires were lit and the smell of woodsmoke mingled on the air with that of potages and boiled vegetables. There was little noise or music for the Puritans discouraged music and dancing, but in a few pockets on the edge of camp a melancholy ballad or two could be heard and some men danced with the women before stealing away to their tents together.

Gabriel Gubbins looked on absently, lost in his thoughts of where Somerset, Klaudia Cay may be.

He was uncomfortable with finding himself where he had been before; although this time he was marching with the New Model Army and not the Royalists. He was sure they were moving towards Naseby and the battle, though no one knew at this point there was even going to be a battle.

All he could do was wait, see if the Voices came to him to give him any clue to the whereabouts of Somerset. Was she coming closer? Would she arrive before the battle and would Time allow them to change course? Before, both of them had become separated on the battlefield, he with the Forlorn Hope of Musketeers and she fighting her own battle with a Time Violator. Gubbins had the strange feeling of history being repeated, the outcome the same. In this he knew he would be shot at the beginning of the battle.

He pushed the thought to one side, thanking a passing soldier who thrust a pewter plate of food and a hunk of bread into his hand. He thanked the man again and stared, gratefully, at the dish before him. Camp food was never good. This was an exception, a platter of stuffed trout, filled with herbs and covered with a thin sauce, the aroma reminding him of home, family and Mary, their cook, and her fine dishes.

He soaked up the juices with the bread and savoured the taste. So much was he enjoying it he had not noticed a girl who was sat on a branch of a fallen tree nearby. Suddenly he became aware of her presence and he leapt to his feet, nearly spilling the plate of good food. Where had she come from?

"You are enjoying the meal?" The girl questioned.

"I made it for you. It is much liked where I come from." Her accent was not one he recognised. For such a young man he was widely travelled around England, the war being fought throughout the land and he, variously, an Intelligencer at times, helping his brother Nathaniel in the 'Cause', the secret society that aimed to bring peace between the King and Cromwell. But he could not place this dark, Spanish-looking girl.

She laughed, flirtatiously, her bodice low enough cut to show a hint of her ample breasts, a bosom Gubbins could barely keep his eyes from. He tore away his gaze to look her squarely in the face while still taking in the shape of her body. A girl, yes, but nearing the fullness of a young woman with curves and a slim waist, the billowing skirt only serving to accentuate her shape.

Her legs would be slender and well-shaped, he was certain of that. Her face held both a look of innocence and, he thought, or perhaps convinced himself, carnal knowledge beyond his experience. High cheekbones, deep brown eyes that fixed his gaze, pouting lips that moved sensuously when she spoke with a lilt in her voice, all cut to his senses. Here was beauty, attraction and though he fought hard to hold back, desire and lust spread like a wave through his body. He was speechless.

"Your friend, Somerset, is fighting hard to reach you, Gabriel Gubbins, though she has many, many miles to travel and there are forces at work tirelessly seeking to stop her. I am sent to tell you this. Be not afeared for her, she is a fighter, you know it is true, and no one could doubt between us all we will see justice prevail." Gubbins looked longingly at the beautiful girl before him and at once he felt she was a Traveller.

***

The first lunge from the soldier before her was clumsy, as if he was inexperienced with the sword. He was no more than a boy. Kat saw he had a pistol in his belt. There was a crossover strap that came from the back of the belt, over the shoulder, like a brace. A slash from her sword severed both this and the belt itself. The pistol dropped to the floor with a clatter on the flagstones but it did not go off. She could see she had cut the man deep but the wound would not be life-threatening. He stared at her for a moment, in disbelief at her speed and skill at fencing, his own attempts foiled in a flash. He turned and ran, first into the street and then towards the Annes' cottage.

Klaudia was bravely fighting the other man, equalling Kat's prowess with a sword she was unfamiliar with. She lunged, parried and thrust her opponent's attempts, forcing him back through the door of the inn and into the street as well. There was a moment when he began to fiercely try to slash his way back into the fight but Klaudia had the measure of him and her sheer speed had him now retreating from her flashing sword. Then one stroke caught his arm and chest. He groaned and staggered back, dropping his own weapon. There was a moment, a second, when it looked as if Klaudia was poised to finish him but he reached with his good hand to the flintlock pistol in his belt. Klaudia was no longer near enough to inflict another wound, she was defenceless against the gun.

Tom Cobbold rode at speed down the street with the horses. He took a pistol from his belt and fired at the man. Klaudia heard the hiss as the lead ball passed. The man was knocked off his feet with the impact, his shoulder blade shattered. Somehow he got up and ran, or rather limped down the street towards the growing Hopkins encampment.

"I had thought we would leave on the 'morrow but now we must go. If what Matthew Hopkins says is true he has authority in these parts and will dispatch his men to follow us." Tom was calming the horses as he spoke.

"Our weapons." I shouted. I grabbed hold of Kat and we ran back into the inn. Madeleine was in tears, leaning against the big oak table by the fireplace. We placed the swords on the table.

"You have to come with us Madeleine." I begged.

"I can not, this is our home, I must stay. I will seek the Justice and tell him of what Hopkins and his men are doing here. It is not right."

"But you must come, don't you see, they will take you away. For everyone they accuse of being a witch they get money. They don't care if you are a witch or not, they will still accuse you."

"I will stay. I have a duty, not just to the inn but to others. It is better I remain here for I can help you, in ways you do not know." That puzzled me and I began to get a strange feeling about Madeleine but before I could dwell on it Tom Cobbold came through the door.

"Why do you wait? They will come for us. Go, get your weapons. Madeleine will be safe, in the protection of the Lords." As we ran up the stairs to the bedroom to retrieve our swords and pistols the word 'Lords' stayed with me. Not Lord, as in God and the Holy Trinity. There is more to this I was thinking when I turned to see another of Hopkins' men in the doorway, aiming a pistol at me. I had no time to raise mine and fire, though I tried.

There was a loud bang and that hissing sound. I tried to dive out of the path of the bullet, but realising in the same awful moment that Kat was behind me. As I hit the floor, about to fire my pistol I saw, almost in slow motion, the front of the soldier's doublet burst open with scarlet and the armoured breast plate left his body with his soul as he fell forwards, his face locked in a grim mask of death. Behind him stood Tom Cobbold, a smoking musket in his hands, fired at close range. I was not happy about this but now we had our own war to fight.

We all ran downstairs, hardly a moment to say goodbye to Madeleine, though Tom held her to him in a hug and said don't worry, we'll be back. I could sense there was something different about Madeleine, almost as if she wasn't of this time but it was a fleeting thought as we ran for the horses, climbed astride the wide saddles and kicked the animals to gallop out of Brandeston. In the distance we could see the Witchfinder General's men mounting up, ready to pursue us.

***

Prince Rupert of the Rhine, to many people, was arrogant and ill tempered. Others saw only a young fellow with a taste for fancy clothes, feathered hats and long, curly hair. To his men, the Royalists fighting for King Charles 1, he was someone they trusted and obeyed. He was tall and thin and this day, as on so many others before battle, he was clad in scarlet, adorned with silver lace and he sat astride a Barbary horse.

At the age of only ten years he had entered university. At fourteen he joined the army in the Low Countries as a commander of a cavalry regiment, fighting the Holy Roman Emperor. Now, as the King's nephew and with his brother Maurice, he had the King's trust. He was firstly appointed his Majesty's Lieutenant-General of Horse, then General of the Army and the King's Military Advisor.

Whilst Gabriel Gubbins was camped with the New Model Army in the siege of Oxford, before moving North to Kislingbury, Prince Rupert had set out with his men from Stow-on-the-Wold in Oxfordshire to ride to a Royalist rendezvous in Leicestershire. They hoped Lord Goring and others would join them.

Goring, who was a difficult man, did agree to join up but on the way some of his soldiers thought they were fighting a Parliamentary patrol when, in fact, they were fighting some of their own men. This delayed him. But Prince Rupert was joined by others and together they all rode for Leicester, a prosperous town of brewers and manufacturers, held by the Roundheads. The Prince and his men surprised some of the Parliamentarians who were out hunting with their Greyhounds. Prince Rupert arrived at the town and demanded the gates be opened.

The townspeople sent out a trumpeter to negotiate terms and ask for time to consult their position. The Prince gave them fifteen minutes to surrender. Two hundred New Model Army Dragoons arrived and the town refused to give in. The Royalists opened fire with their cannons and in a few hours blew holes in the walls.

Prince Rupert and the Cavalry rode into the town and plundered it, taking a thousand muskets and five hundred barrels of gunpowder. This attack on Leicester caused the Roundheads to recall General Fairfax from his siege of Oxford and so the New Model Army marched north. Oliver Cromwell was on the way from Huntingdon to join the rest of the army, which was now nearly twice the size of the King's.

And so Gabriel Gubbins found himself with the Roundhead army but at the moment he only had thoughts for the pretty young woman before him. She was older than him and, he sensed, very mature. Until now his only real contact with girls of his age had been when he rode with Somerset but he had never seen Klaudia in the same light as this and he did not trust his senses. Except for one, his intuition, and the difference in this girl was beginning to dawn on him.

"You are a Traveller. Am I correct in this?"

"I am, Sir, and I have had a moment in Time to bring you the message I have told you, that Klaudia is coming to you as we speak."

"Tell me, what is your name and where are you from?" Gubbins had barely issued the words when all he saw before him was the fallen branch and in a wisp, as if never there, the girl had gone.

11
BURY ST. EDMUNDS

They were big horses, the ones we were riding out of the village of Brandeston, with Hopkins' men hard on our heels. I wished I had more speed and that the saddles were not so big and heavy, with saddle bags loaded with provisions and ammunition. There were muskets in the scabbards and now we had our own pistols and swords we were well armed.

Tom Cobbold knew the countryside and he led the way along the course of the river until we reached a bridge which, once we had crossed it, gave us cover. He pulled his horse up sharp and told us to get down behind the stone parapet as he took out his musket. He rested the weapon on the wall of the bridge and took aim.

Now muskets are not that accurate unless you really know what you're doing. I could sense Tom was an expert and had done this many times before. His confidence was obvious as he smiled at me before turning to sight the musket and fire at the oncoming riders. I saw one man taken clean off his horse. The others halted and quickly turned. I had not noticed until then that Tom had taken my musket from its scabbard and now he fired that one as well.

Although he did not hit anyone this time, as they were riding back out of range, it was another warning to them and gave us enough time to mount up and ride towards a distant hill covered with woods. Here we rode into the trees for cover and we could see in the distance Hopkins and his men had rallied but no one had seen where we had turned off the road and they moved on in the wrong direction. We kicked our horses into a trot and made our way across country to Bury St. Edmunds.

We came into the bustle of the market town. It was market day and the street sellers had set up their stalls or were walking around with baskets of produce balanced on their heads. Some were shouting their wares.

"Radishes or lettis two bunches a penny."

"New mackrell, lily white mussels."

"Buy my hartichokes nistris."

"White St. Thomas onions."

"Fine oranges or lemons," and "I have fresh cheese and creams." They all competed to be heard which made the place very noisy. Not all of them were selling food. Others were selling buttons and there was a knife grinder with the grinding wheel and a foot treadle to operate it, all mounted into a wheelbarrow.

We rode between people and carriages, others on horses, some rich people being carried in sedan chairs supported by chairmen. Tom Cobbold told us it was a way the rich, apart from being carried around the town, could avoid having rubbish and the contents of chamber pots thrown down on them. People did this, just throwing their rubbish out of windows into the street below. I felt sorry for the chairmen who got stuff thrown on them.

As we came into the market square we saw some women wearing big, floppy hats and gowns over brocade skirts. Others had petticoats and waistcoats and many were carrying shopping baskets they were filling with fruit, vegetables and fish.

"Housewives and servants come to shop for their households." Tom explained. There were stalls selling food and ale, morris dancers and men wearing costumes that made their bottom halves look like they were riding horses as part of the dance. Children imitated them on their own hobby horses they had been bought from street vendors. One man was collecting money for the morris performers and some men and women stood looking on. They were finely dressed and rich-looking in contrast to the bustling women with their baskets.

Dogs ran around freely, barking at the dancers, and the air was smelly. Kat looked at me and pulled a face. I had to laugh as I had seen things like this before in Oxford and Thame where people walked around with nosegays to cover the smell of rotting vegetables and human waste in the streets. We found our way to the bishop's palace, which was not really like a big palace or anything, it was more like part of an abbey. We left our horses with a hostler in a courtyard.

The bishop was a kindly old man and he was very disturbed to hear of what happened in Brandeston and to the vicar. We were sitting in his parlour and he had read the letter of introduction from the vicar. He looked gravely again at the letter and then prepared papers for us to give us safe passage.

"You look like Royalist musketeers," he remarked, "there are parts of the Royalist army marching west at present. You will be wise to join them for Cromwell and his men are not far away, travelling in the same direction."

Towards Naseby, I was thinking.

"It would be best if you were to leave Bury for the

road since, from what you tell me, the Witchfinder General and his men will not be long behind you and the city has many eyes and ears spying for him. Keep south of Cambridge. There are Royalists in the area and you can join up with them." We thanked the bishop and returned to the horses which were recovering from our ride to Bury. They had been given water and food. I thought we would ride straight out of Bury but Tom said we had one more stop. It was then I remembered we had more papers of introduction to the Magistrate, which would give us safe passage in Roundhead areas.

We picked our way back through the bustling market place and across to the court house. There was a really big wagon, a haywain piled high with straw, parked in front of the building, as well as some carriages and several horses tied up but unattended. There was a soldier at the entrance who barred our way at first but Tom produced the vicar's letter and explained we were there to see the magistrate. The man let us pass and an usher took us upstairs to a large room on the first floor. Kat and I watched as Tom Cobbold paced around the room.

There was a long table and a few chairs. One, at the centre of the table, was very ornate in Jacobean style, with candy twists and tapestry cushions. We had some like that at home. A stream of sunlight entered the room through a stained glass window that almost filled a whole wall, casting coloured light across the table and floor. We did not have to wait long because in walked the Magistrate with Matthew Hopkins and his men. The bishop was right, we should have left Bury straight away.

"Are these the ones you accuse of breaking the law

in Brandeston?" The Magistrate looked to Hopkins.

"They are, sir, they acted to prevent the apprehension of a suspected witch. We have the request of the good people of Brandeston to find witches amongst them, as indeed we do in the towns and villages thereabouts. We have the seal of the Justices themselves to find and bring to trial those who practice maleficium and witchcraft."

"Rightly so, and how many have you apprehended so far?"

"Twenty three were tried at Chelsmford and nineteen hanged. We list eighteen we believe will come to the Justices at Bury for trial, if it please your Lordship. It is the will of God."

"Then we can begin with these three, though not accused of witchcraft they have sought to aid and abet witches and attempt to murder some of your good men, from what you tell me. Tie them to the chairs." The Magistrate motioned to some soldiers who had entered the room. Now I felt the anger rising up and I was not going to stand for this. I looked at Tom Cobbold and Kat and we all three nodded in agreement. All for one I was thinking. No one had taken away our swords or pistols. Tom Cobbold leaped onto a chair and in one movement across and onto the long table, towering over the Magistrate who had sat down in the ornate chair. Tom pulled his pistol from his belt and fired at the head of Matthew Hopkins.

The bullet blew the man's hat off his head and he looked shocked. Kat and I had drawn our swords and we joined Tom on the table, fencing the soldiers from aloft. They kept slicing to hit our legs but we jumped over their swords and we edged our way along the table.

The Magistrate had a look of complete disbelief that this could be happening in his court house.

Suddenly Tom Cobbold shouted to us to follow and he ran along the table and took what I thought was a big leap of faith, crashing through the stained glass window. It gave way easily and he disappeared. Kat and I took the same faith and followed him through.

We dropped from the first floor onto the haywain below, landing in soft straw. We jumped down into the muddy street and ran for the bishop's palace and to the horses, following Tom. Now I am a champion runner and Kat is pretty fit too. We easily overtook Tom, at least we thought we had, but looking back I saw he had stopped. The soldiers had appeared at the door of the court house. Tom shouted to us to get the horses as he aimed his pistol at the soldiers and fired. It was a warning shot, I could tell because it did not drop anyone, just splintered the doorframe. I ran on and found Kat with the hostler and the horses ready.

We mounted and led the horses out of the courtyard, riding up to Tom who had his second pistol pointed at the doorway. I handed him the reins and he got on his horse. I had pulled out the musket I had in my saddle scabbard but Tom laid a hand on my arm and pointed at the court house. The soldiers had retreated inside. I put the gun back and we rode out into the market. People were shaking their fists and some threw vegetables at us.

Our horses barged their way through the stalls, knocking some flying and sending fruit rolling into the mud. A poor woman with a basket of fish on her head tripped and fell, tipping the fish into the chaos of running feet, with people trying to escape the market square as Tom fired a shot in the air. I felt bad about this but we had to push our way through to make our escape because it was happening again. Matthew Hopkins and his men had appeared and were mounting up. They were coming after us.

Tom led us fast through the streets of Bury St. Edmunds and it was obvious he knew where he was going. We sensed that Hopkins was closing the gap as the way had been cleared by our rapid progress through the streets with people throwing themselves to one side, away from the path of thundering hooves on cobble stones. We reached the edge of town but instead of taking to the road Tom led us onto a track which took us around the side of a hill and there ahead was an entrance to chalk tunnels built into a big mound. We rode straight in, dismounted and quietened the horses, holding our breath. Tom reloaded his pistols as we waited for Hopkins to appear.

We had heard from the bishop in Bury that Oliver Cromwell and his men had set out from Huntingdon and were aiming to join the main New Model Army. It had left the siege of Oxford to march north and retake Leicester that had fallen to Prince Rupert of the Rhine and the King's troops. I was still thinking if somehow we could get to Naseby before the battle started we could make things different. I didn't mean to mess with Time but could we, in some way help to change things for the better, find Gubbins and get to Parliament to petition against the Witchfinder General? He seemed to have it all his own way in Essex, Suffolk and Norfolk, with Parliament and everyone so involved in the war.

No one in Bury, apart from the bishop, knew where we were heading, or so we thought.

"See, they know not we are here." Tom pointed to the riders in the distance, on the road back to Brandeston. It was definitely Hopkins and it looked as if they had given up the chase. Time would lead us to a different conclusion but for now we had the chance to leave Bury St. Edmunds. We rode out of the chalk caves and started an arduous ride away from the town, choosing to go across country and taking short cuts where we could, much to the anger of some farmers as we rode through their crops. They shouted abuse at us.

It was getting late and we would have to find somewhere to stay or sleep rough. I was not sure which was best or worst. If we stayed at an inn people could talk, telling that we had passed that way. We couldn't be really sure whether or not Hopkins had sent anyone after us. On the other hand, we had money and money talks too. To sleep rough was dangerous because there were military patrols out hunting for deserters, spies, the enemy, whatever.

Late afternoon saw us riding for Cambridge but we had to slow the pace as the horses were getting blown. No one said much. I realised we had not eaten for hours and felt really hungry. My other thoughts were with what we had left behind us. A trail of havoc and now we were wanted by the Magistrates.

We couldn't ever go back to Bury. I wondered how we would get back to Brandeston and find Kat's Grimoire. Poor Tom Cobbold. What would he do when this was over? I was thinking ahead too. How would the Time Thing work when I had been at Naseby before? Now the circumstances were different. I was sure I couldn't be in two places at the same time. Or could I? Another question. Had we escaped from Hopkins? We were not to know he had been torturing the two Annes and the vicar and knew more than we thought. Tom told us he knew some innkeepers in Cambridge from his days as a smuggler when he supplied them with illicit alcohol, no questions asked. That couldn't have been more than a year ago, I thought, given his age. I was thinking back as well to what Madeleine had said about Gubbins. What did she know? Who was she really? And so we came to Cambridge and we only had a few days left before the Battle of Naseby.

***

There was an atmosphere in the Roundhead camp that you could cut with a knife. Riders came and went, carrying despatches and bringing news of the whereabouts of King Charles 1 and his army. The word was that the Royalists were marching south to return to Oxford and relieve the city.

Gabriel Gubbins had the advantage of knowing there would be a battle in just a few days time but he could not say anything to the soldiers of the New Model Army. Anyway, who would believe he had travelled back from 1647, the year that saw the King disappear from Hampton Court? Gubbins did not dwell on this, indeed, his thoughts as he awoke in his tent the following morning were of the strange girl who had appeared the night before, and disappeared just as quickly as she came. Whose food he had partaken and who had stirred in him feelings he had not previously experienced.

Word came that Oliver Cromwell was arriving from Huntingdon with his cavalry. A rider from Northampton rode into camp to say Cromwell was expected there soon. The officers continued to send out scouts to learn more of the King's position. The New Model Army was joining up, the camp swelling with soldiers and soon would reach thirteen thousand five hundred fighting men. Infantry, cavalry and dragoons. Gubbins was part of the infantry. As a Musketeer in the Forlorn Hope of Musketeers he would be one of the first to face the enemy, the Royalists. Muskets had a range of three hundred yards but were only accurate at about fifty yards.

So the Musketeers would form a barrier of fire and, most likely, be the first to go down in the battle. Gubbins, already a handsome young fellow with a shock of fair hair contrasting his tanned face, looked splendid in his New Model Army uniform. His red jacket with yellow lining, seen at the collar and where the cuffs were turned back, was crossed by his yellow shoulder belt for his sword and a bandoleer from which hung 'Twelve Apostles', the blue leather tubes each of which contained a measured charge of gunpowder.

The front rim of his big, floppy hat, was tied back to keep it out of his face. His breeches were grey with buttons down the front and came to just below his knees to meet his 'stockins' and brown Roundhead boots. He had in his hand a soldier's waxed leather Snapsack which contained a bowl and cup, his Strike-a-Light set for arming his musket, a knife, spoon, and spare stockins. For now, his jacket buttons were undone as he set out across the camp to find some bread and cheese. A group of soldiers, infantry Pike men, approached him. One spoke.

"We hear there are Royalists near Daventry, an outpost for the King, we are told. Do you think we do battle soon?"

"Aye, it will not be long if the King's army is close. Oliver Cromwell is not far away," Gubbins answered "it is said he is in the mood for a fight, as is Sir Thomas Fairfax."

"Then it is muskets and pikes at the ready." Another fellow said.

"Would it be that we were cavalry, my feet are sore hurt from all the marching." Gubbins had a cheeky look and the others laughed at this. They moved off to find food, leaving Gubbins chewing on his piece of bread and cheese, with a cup of ale to wash it down. His thoughts returned to the girl of the night before and he wondered if he would ever see her again.

12
THE GREEN MAN

Tom Cobbold had decided we would avoid going into Cambridge itself because of the strong Puritan and Roundhead presence. Oliver Cromwell himself had been Member of Parliament for Cambridge. I asked Tom if it was wise to even go near Cambridge but he replied that the inn we would stay at would be safe. We rode through a ford across the river Cam and came to Grantchester Meadows. The meadows and the village were very picturesque and you could almost forget we were in the middle of a civil war. Cambridge in the distance was like a backdrop and I was reminded of Oxford. How I wanted to go home and I felt for Kat. At least I had travelled before and knew something of what to expect. She gave me a look that said she was more comfortable with it, being with Tom Cobbold.

"We will stop at The Green Man. Don't worry, we are safe here and I wish to collect money owed to me, for the journey." We rode up to the inn which was on the edge of the meadows and dropped out of our saddles. Now I am pretty fit and so is Kat but we're not used to riding for so long. My legs were shaky. I thought I might fall over. We tied the horses near a water trough so they could drink and went into the inn. Now I know my legs were weak but you could have knocked me over with a feather because the girl at the bar was Madeleine. How could it be? How could she have got here, even in the time we were in Bury?

"He is safe, Klaudia, with the Parliamentary army and a handsome young man he is too, your Gabriel Gubbins." She smiled. A shudder went right through me and I was trying to grasp what she was saying. How could she know? Unless.

"You're a Traveller."

"That is right and true."

"And you've seen Gabriel?" I don't know why but my mind was running away with all sorts of weird thoughts. She called him 'my' Gabriel Gubbins, like he was my boyfriend or something. I had never thought of Gabriel like that. I mean, I had had lots of boyfriends, well two actually, but I didn't count Gubbins as one. He was a friend I rode with in 1647 and together we saved the King and Oliver Cromwell from assassination. Madeleine. A Traveller. I knew there was something different about her and then I suddenly felt jealous. She had seen Gubbins. She being older than me and very pretty and, well, you know, well developed and everything.

"Where is he?" I stuttered.

"Some miles yet from Naseby, in a Roundhead camp on the road from Oxford. I took him some trout after you left Brandeston. He really liked it." I looked at her sharply. Now I was feeling a bit angry. How could she do that and not say anything. Didn't she have to have a Caller to travel? Am I the only one? I am supposed to be a Time Princess and I seem to be the only one who can't just travel when she wants to.

Tom Cobbold sensed the tension in the air and I could almost see what Kat was thinking. I calmed myself down. I seem to be getting pretty good at that these days. Madeleine produced tankards of ale for us and we gratefully sipped the beer, only then realising how thirsty the ride had made us. I had lots of questions brewing but once again Tom seemed to know of them before I could ask.

"The Green Man is another of our inns, we have several in our family," he stated in a matter of fact sort of way. "We could stay here but we must be careful of patrols. We can eat and be refreshed." After the day we'd had that seemed like the best thing and all I wanted to add was sleep. There were no customers in the inn, not yet, though I suppose it was early. The striking of a clock told me it was five o'clock. Madeleine disappeared into the kitchen and re-emerged carrying a tray with a big pie. I started to salivate and I could see Kat was looking longingly at the dish.

"What is it made from? She whispered to me.

"Don't ask." I said. "This is 1645 and they cook things a bit differently. Eat it. I promise it won't poison you." She took a portion and tucked in. My first taste told me what I had already thought. In this dish they took the heart, liver, kidney and other innards of a deer and combined it with apples, currants, sugar and spices and baked it as a pie. It had a name from the old English for a deer's innards: numble. And so it became known as numble pie and because it was eaten by people who weren't rich (the rich would get the venison) it got another name. This wasn't the first time I had eaten Humble Pie.

As we were eating people began to arrive in the inn but they didn't seem too interested in us. They were dressed like clerics and learned people and I worked out they must be from the University, academics, who looked to be in their own world and not bothered by some boys who were dressed as Royalist musketeers. I wanted to talk to Madeleine, to find out more from her about Gubbins but she was busy at the tables and I never did get the chance. A Roundhead patrol walked in and this time we slipped quietly out of the bar, through the kitchen and up some back stairs to the bedrooms.

Tom Cobbold acted like a real gentleman and showed us the room, saying we would be safe there for the night. There was only one bed but it was a four poster, draped with tapestries and big enough for Kat and me to sleep in. Tom quietly closed the door as he left the room and we sat side by side on the bed. Kat's eyes were welling up and I felt a bit emotional as well. It had been quite a journey, through time and now to here, Grantchester Meadows. We didn't really know where next, only that we had to find Gabriel Gubbins.

"You won't leave me, will you Klaudia? I mean, I'm scared of being stuck here and not able to get home." Kat gave a little sob and I put my arm round her to console her.

"Of course I won't leave you, we're mates and we are going to get through this together. With Tom Cobbold's and Gubbins' help we'll get back your Grimoire. We'll petition Parliament to put an end to witch hunts and then we'll go home. No one will have missed us, in our time it will have been only a few seconds we were gone." Even as I was saying the words there were some doubts in my mind. I made it all sound too easy and life is not like that. First, we had to get to Naseby. I knew Gabriel was fighting on the Roundhead side and here we were dressed as Royalist musketeers. I suppose I should have said something to Madeleine when she gave us the clothes to wear. But the wardrobe seemed to only have Cavalier style clothes. Tom Cobbold was no Puritan, that was for sure. His family looked to be pretty rich, with the inns and everything. They must have made money as pirates I thought. I did remember Tom saying something about the Spanish Main and Tortuga. How they had brought a load of silver taken from a Spanish ship. But when I had asked him to tell me more about his exploits he had fallen silent and just shrugged, saying it was all war, everywhere was a war.

Kat and I hung our bandoleers over a chair and took off the layers of clothing, including the leather jackets designed to help protect from sword cuts. It felt good to get out of the boys' clothes. We tumbled into the four poster and almost immediately fell asleep. The last sound I heard as I drifted off was the barking of a dog fox.

The morning brought a mist drifting across the meadows and somewhere a lark was singing, waking us to a new day. Kat said she needed to pee and I looked around for a chamber pot but couldn't find one, which was unusual. I thought I would go and find Madeleine and ask her to give us one. I opened the door and, as if she knew what I was thinking, she was standing there.

"There's no chamber pot, we need to, you know..." I tailed off. She smiled and pointed to another door. I opened it and looked in. There was a proper latrine, with a seat and a hole for the 'night soil'. That was a surprise because earth closets were usually outside. There was no toilet paper of course. I knew sometimes you would get a piece of lace or wool but instead there was a pile of political pamphlets all torn up ready to use. I pointed Kat towards the latrine. Now was my opportunity to question Madeleine. I sensed she was a Traveller.

"How did you see Gubbins? You must be a Traveller. How do you do that?"

"We are from a Gypsy family, part Irish, part Spanish. I have the power to travel. You are a Traveller too, Klaudia. I know it is how you came to be here. Your friend Gubbins is like us. You have great power, I sense it, though you do not know how to use it to the full. I can move around in my own time. It is how I came to see Gubbins as you were on the way to Bury St. Edmunds. I told him you were trying to reach him and he seemed to take some solace in that. I was there only briefly before I came here to The Green Man."

"Why are you and Tom helping us in this way? What do you want with us?"

"Only to see the end of the Witchfinder General. It was he who was the cause of our mother's suffering and demise in Manningtree, when she was accused of witchcraft. She was a Traveller too, but not a witch." It was becoming clear to me they wanted revenge for their mother's death. No wonder Tom Cobbold had no hesitation in shooting Matthew Hopkins' men. I did not have a problem with this.

I was feeling hungry again and I wondered what we would find for breakfast. Madeleine couldn't tell me any more about Gubbins, unless she was keeping some things to herself. She went downstairs to the kitchen as we got dressed in our Cavalier clothes, leaving our blue jackets in our room and going to breakfast wearing shirts, breeches and boots. It appeared there was no one staying at the inn as Tom Cobbold walked in and we piled our pewter plates with cold meats, butter and bread. There was white wine or tea to drink. Tom said he had readied the horses so we could get on the road quickly and find a Royalist troop we could join up with. At least we had the bishop's papers for safe passage even if we had not managed to get the ones for Roundhead areas.

And so we set off, across the misty Grantchester Meadows which were peaceful and quiet and a place where you wanted to stay, drawn like a magnet to the tranquillity. The mist began to clear as we rode and now we were heading for Bedford and on to Northampton. From there we would ride for Naseby. Keeping this far south we should be well away from Oliver Cromwell's troops further north.

The horses were rested and fresh, in good spirits, snorting and neighing as they caught the morning air. Madeleine had packed food for lunch into the saddle bags so there was no need to draw attention to ourselves by stopping in any of the villages we passed through. Country people, those not signed up to the Cavaliers or Roundhead armies, worked the land and we saw many of them gaze enviously at our horses. Often, they were using bullocks to pull ploughs. We observed only a few big Suffolk Punches doing the job. June sunshine burned off the rest of the mist and we were making good progress, but getting hot in our jackets and layers of clothes.

It reached midday and we stopped on the edge of a village near the river Cam. Usually at this time in the 1640's you would have dinner and if you were rich there would be lots of dishes of food. We had with us a sort of smaller version with some meat, game, sweets and cheese that Madeleine had packed for us. We were glad to take off our jackets and cool down. The horses were grazing on the side of the track and we sat on the grass. For the first time since we had left Brandeston, Kat was smiling and chatting happily to Tom Cobbold, almost as if we were on a picnic in our own time. I wondered when we would be back home.

There was a single shot of a musket and a ball hissed over our heads, hitting the stone of the nearby bridge, disintegrating into shards of hot metal. It was a warning shot. Tom put his hand on my arm as I reached for a pistol. Kat's hand was on her sword. Tom said wait, be still. If whoever took the shot had wanted to kill us they could have by now.

I suppose we were silly, we were sitting targets, literally, and as it turned out, because we had taken off our jackets in the heat of the sun, the troop of soldiers could not tell if we were friend or foe. Thankfully, as it turned out, they were Royalist soldiers, Cavaliers, and one of the troops we had hoped to find to continue on our journey. What became very clear, though, was there was a problem in meeting them, as you will see.

13
ROYALISTS

King Charles 1's Intelligencers had informed him that the Roundheads' New Model Army, led by General Fairfax, was nearing Daventry. The Cavaliers decided to withdraw to Market Harborough, taking plunder and cattle as they went. Jack Ashburnham, a Groom of the Bedchamber for the King, had the King's attention and he wanted the Royalists to fight. Prince Rupert was not so keen. He wanted to wait for Lord Goring to arrive with his troops.

Charles Gerrard, who was one of the Cavaliers' best cavalry commanders, was also on his way with his troopers. Joined together the King's army would be at full strength to defeat the Roundheads' New Model Army. But like Lord Goring, Gerrard got delayed as well.

In the Roundhead camp Gabriel Gubbins took it as a sign when a rider, a spy for Cromwell, rode in with a letter. It was from Lord Goring to Prince Rupert and had been intercepted. In the letter Lord Goring said he could not get to the King for some time, being delayed in the West Country. The camp began preparations to move on the King whose position had been reported. Now Gubbins was certain the battle would take place and he steadied himself for the unfolding of the Battle of Naseby.

***

The leader of the Royalist troopers was a Sergeant who, on looking at our papers, was satisfied we were on his side. We gathered everything up into our saddle bags and followed the riders into the village where there were more Royalists, one of whom was a Cavalier whose name was Captain Dagger. Now this is the scary part. I had met Captain Dagger before but I realised he would not recognise me. Although, when I had met him I was dressed like now, as a boy, today was before I had met him in a previous Time Trip. That was weird but time travel is full of strange little tricks.

While Captain Dagger was examining our papers, I noticed there were some men in manacles and others with their hands tied by ropes. Roundhead prisoners, I was sure. We were all standing outside the village inn and there were a lot of Cavaliers drinking ale, making jokes and laughing. There was a big, hoop covered wagon with two Suffolk Punches standing patiently.

What happened next was really bad for us but for now there was nothing we could do about it. Captain Dagger took away our horses, just as had happened to Gubbins although, of course, I did not know that. Dagger said we would get them back later but for now there were officers without horses who would ride them, and they would go ahead while we marched. That would slow us down.

We were allowed to keep our muskets and were made to march with the Musketeers and infantrymen in the troop. Worse still, we were not marching for Naseby. Captain Dagger's orders were to march to Chinnor, in Oxfordshire, where the prisoners would be held in a gaol. Then to Oxford to help relieve the city and protect it until the King arrived with Prince Rupert and the army. Captain Dagger would not listen when we told him Oliver Cromwell was riding from Huntingdon to join up with the New Model Army. Neither would he believe there was to be a battle because, as he put it, Cromwell would not dare and the King would return to Oxford with the army.

We began marching, going south towards Oxford. Our chance of getting to Gubbins before the battle was now starting to slip away with every step we took. We needed a plan.

Tom Cobbold spread the map on the ground. We had stopped marching and were setting up camp for the night. I had overheard Captain Dagger and the Sergeant discussing sending the mounted officers ahead in the morning. On our horses. We had to do something. The Infantrymen had blankets, food and their personal things in their knapsacks but the tents were carried in the wagon and now they started unloading them.

This was my opportunity to retrieve the map from my saddlebag and I found the horses in a makeshift compound. I managed to get the map undetected and now we were looking at the distance we had to travel to get to Naseby. If we could get away on our horses tonight we might just make it in time, before the battle.

The Royalist men were putting up the tents and one man was handing out ale. Everyone seemed in good spirits and another man began to sing, a sad ballad of love lost in war. Although it was sad, the Cavaliers joined in the chorus and there were lots of happy faces. That was probably the ale. Apart from Captain Dagger's and the Sergeant's, ours were the only other horses and we decided we were going to take them back. We would escape and even though we were sure Captain Dagger and the Sergeant would come after us, we had to take the risk. We also had the element of surprise. It was a question of when we could get the horses and bolt. It proved to be surprisingly easy as the men had more ale and Captain Dagger retired to his tent. The Sergeant was drinking with his men, propping himself up on his halberd, the axe on a pole that he and men of his rank carried into battle. More singing and the ballads were getting bawdier and risqué. Tom signalled to us and we crept around the back of the tents to the horse compound.

Thankfully no one had, as yet, removed the saddles from our horses and we were able to lead them quietly to the edge of the compound without anyone seeing us. We hoped. We were just about to mount up when an Infantry man appeared, unbuttoning his trousers to take a pee, when he spotted us.

"Ho, what are you about?" He called.

"Just getting our food from our saddle bags, that is all." Tom replied for all of us. The man stumbled off to find another place to relieve himself and we climbed into the saddles, leading the Captain's and the Sergeant's horses with us out of the compound. We had decided to take them with us until we were far enough away that they could not catch up, but near enough they would find the horses. No one could accuse us of stealing our own horses but we did not want to be labelled horse thieves by the Royalists. So we stole away into the night, leaving their horses a little way down the road. We did hear shouting a short while later but that could have been the men in continuing good spirits with their ale.

It was a clear night with a bright moon and plenty of stars. Tom said we would ride on, guided by the stars and I realised of course, he was a buccaneer and could tell we were going in the right direction according to the position of the stars in the celestial sky. We decided to ride well south of Bedford to avoid more patrols.

Eventually though, I thought we must find somewhere to rest, if not sleep, or both we and the horses would not get far the following day. We did stop when we stumbled across a half-built wooden barn on what appeared to be the edge of a country estate. We could see the silhouette of an abbey in the distance, the moonlight shining on it, giving it an eerie effect.

The barn had a roof and three walls and was part-filled with hay. A big, empty haywain was nearby and we tied the horses to it. We each found a place in the hay and very quickly fell asleep, trusting that in this remote place we would be safe for a few hours until we could ride on.

I awoke to find myself being poked by a pitchfork. Kat was still asleep nearby but from the position I was in I could not see Tom Cobbold. I was staring up at the face of a very handsome fellow. He must have been about twenty-five or so. He had long, brown curly hair that parted in the middle and tumbled to his shoulders. Not a look I usually like but on him it was looking good. His white shirt was open at the chest and I could see he was fit, well-muscled. I was about to reach for the pistol in my belt but where the pitchfork was pressing into me gave me second thoughts.

"Are you deserters?" He asked.

"No sir, we are soldiers detached from our troop, on the way to join the King's army at Naseby." I rallied. Suddenly he lifted the pitchfork and flipped off my hat, causing my hair to tumble down, as long as his, and I saw a look of surprise on his face. Kat had stirred and he turned to her, doing the same to her hat. Her long, blond hair fell about her shoulders as well.

"You are girls. What trickery is this?"

"None, Sir. True, we are girls but we do travel to the King. We are Intelligencers for the Cause, carrying a message for the King's eyes only. We are disguised as boys so as not to bring attention to ourselves as we travel." I can be inventive when I need to.

"Drop the pitchfork, very slowly and then raise your hands up behind your head. One wrong move and this pistol will take you to your god." Tom Cobbold stood behind the man, the pistol pressed firmly into his back. The pitchfork was dropped and the man put his hands up as commanded.

"Look, you are on my Lord's land. I care not if you are deserters or are really on the way to the King but you are trespassing on his land, sleeping in his barn. It is against the law and it is my duty to protect the estate."

"Who is your Lord?" Tom asked him.

"Lord William Russell, Earl of Bedford."

"Ah, the Duke who sided with the Parliamentarians, then with the King, then with the Parliamentarians again. I have heard of him. Whose side is he on now?"

"He is retired from the politics. Parliament refused to allow him to return to his seat in the House of Lords. He wants no further part in the war." The fellow turned to look sheepishly at Tom Cobbold.

"And you would be?"

"I am Thomas Jones, gamekeeper for the Woburn estate." When he said Woburn I suddenly realised where we were. In my time it's where the safari park is, at Woburn Abbey.

"Well, Thomas Jones, you can thank his Lordship for his hospitality in letting us sleep in his barn or, as I suspect you will, say nothing of our presence. You have not seen me, much less the two 'boys' I travel with, lest any who follow ask such questions. Do I have your understanding? A life for a life. We will spare you yours in exchange for silence." Tom Cobbold said firmly. I could see the fellow casted a glance towards Woburn Abbey in the distance, as if he was willing some assistance to appear from there but none did. He gave us a resigned look and shrugged his shoulders.

"May God go with you." Was all he said as he shuffled off. I still thought he looked pretty fit and I could see Kat did too. We untied the horses, mounted up and set off again on our quest to Naseby. By avoiding Bedford and the patrols we had found ourselves much further to the south than intended and needing to make up time.

We rode at a steady pace, the horses again rested and lively. I began thinking what if history had changed and there is no Battle of Naseby? How would we find Gubbins? In hope, I put that to the back of my mind. Besides, Madeleine had claimed she had seen Gubbins near Naseby. If there was no battle we could go to the Haseleys in Oxfordshire, to Manor Farm where Gubbins lived. The house which would become ours three hundred and sixty years later. Kat interrupted my thoughts.

"Klaudia, what will we do when we get to Naseby, how will we find Gubbins, with the battle and everything?"

"Last time, when I travelled back, I found him with the Roundheads' Forlorn Hope of Musketeers before the battle started."

"But we're dressed as Cavalier Musketeers, with our blue jackets." Kat reminded us.

"True, Klaudia, said Tom Cobbold, "the Roundheads will see us from a mile away."

"Gubbins has a brother, Nathaniel, who is an Intelligencer for the Cause. I found him last time with the King's army but he has special papers that let him move between the Cavaliers and the Roundheads. When I was here before he got me through to meet Gubbins."

"If there is to be a battle, do you think you can persuade Gubbins to leave the battlefield and come with us?" Asked Tom. I had not thought about that. To leave before the fight would make Gubbins a deserter. I realised we were not in a good position. Perhaps the Lords Temporal could help.

A Time Shift might put us at Naseby before Gubbins goes into battle with the Forlorn Hope. I tried hard to send that message to the Lords but nothing happened. I am sure they must have known nothing was happening and why but there seemed to be no way to reach them. All my thoughts about getting Kat and me back to our own time had met with no response. We were on our own, apart from Tom Cobbold of course. We rode as straight as we could for Northampton and hoped we could get round the town without meeting any patrols. We were riding into the unknown.

***

Oliver Cromwell had led his cavalry troops from Huntingdon directly for Northampton. He had been made Lieutenant General of the Roundhead army again and he rode solemnly contemplating the possible outcome of yet another potential battle with the King. It was as if no one remembered why the war had started, although Cromwell knew, deep down, it was about many things but money and religion were at the root and never far from being blamed as the cause. That and the fact that King Charles 1 had locked Parliament out of Westminster, for many years before the war began, and tried to rule the country on his own.

Cromwell had tired of the conflict, having fought many battles and tried many times to come to terms with the King. Now, he decided, would be a good time for all to reach a deciding point and end the bloody war. He had received word that General Fairfax's leading detachment of horse had skirmished with the Royalists outposts near Daventry just the day before. So the King knew the Roundheads were in the area and the Royalists, who were trying to join reinforcements at Newark, were at Market Harborough, a few miles north of the village of Naseby.

The New Model Army called a Council of War and there were loud cheers when they were joined by Oliver Cromwell and his troops. It was June 13, 1645 and the Roundheads sent scouts into Naseby where they surprised a Royalist patrol drinking ale at the village inn.

***

Matthew Hopkins, Witchfinder General and his men, having been unsuccessful in apprehending the three young Cavaliers at Bury St. Edmunds, returned swiftly to Brandeston. His camp of followers was growing around the witch hunts and he had with him the girl called Jac who had appeared one day, as if from nowhere, when he was interrogating the witch Mary Clowes of Yoxford. It was Jac who had informed him of the two young girls staying with Mother Leech and Anne Wright. She knew Klaudia would follow her through time. Witches all, she told him, sent from another time to stop his pursuit, condemnation and execution of the witches of all England and Scotland. She had told him as well of the book they had with them. The very book he was looking for. A Grimoire so full of secrets its power might be beyond the comprehension of ordinary mortals.

In the hands of the Witchfinder General it could unleash a power hitherto unseen in the world. Matthew Hopkins had no reason to doubt what this young girl told him. He had heard the Voice of God tell him she had travelled through time to bring him this news.

Very little was known about Hopkins and where he came from and he intended to keep it that way. Some said he had practised as a lawyer, others that he had lived in Holland awhile and learned of witch hunts there and in Germany. To the authorities he had just seemed to appear and start his campaign against witches in Manningtree.

The war did little to appease the rise of the Witchfinder General who had fast become like a law unto himself. Fear in villages and towns, fear of witches and what they could manifest upon innocent people was his ally in his scouring the countryside in search of those who possessed magik. He would hunt witches and end their ability to move from time to time, from century to century, spreading their witchcraft. He would 'end the practise of magik.' Now he was also certain that the two witches Jac had spoken of were indeed two of the Cavaliers he hunted, girls disguised as boys. The third, the one they called Tom Cobbold, seemed familiar, at least the name did but Hopkins could not remember why. No matter, they would not get far and he would bring them to trial for witchcraft, once he has in possession of the book, the Grimoire.

It was an easy matter for Hopkins and his assistant, John Stearne, to extract confessions from Mother Leech and Anne Wright. For witches they were both young, and by that they were resilient at first but Hopkins' form of torture, sleep deprivation, walking them up and down all through the night, soon had them pleading for mercy. Especially when, aided by a smiling Jac, in front of observers from the village of Bandeston, they began 'pricking' them again with needles.

Exhausted from their ordeal they confessed to being witches and to the whereabouts of the young girls who had appeared in Brandeston. Anne Wright sobbed uncontrollably as she revealed the ones called Klaudia and Kat were riding for Naseby to find a Gabriel

Gubbins whose family might influence Parliament to put an end to witchhunting.

Mother Leech proved harder to break, even with torture but Hopkins was not called Witchfinder General without substance. In just a few months he and Stearne had sent to the gallows more people than all the witchunters in one hundred and sixty years of persecution in England. Keeping the witches awake would call their Imps into view and cause the women to confess their allegiance with Satan himself.

Eventually, breaking down in tears, Mother Leech also confessed to practicing the art of magik and that she had handed Kat's Grimoire to John Lowes, Vicar of Brandeston, though she protested she knew not of its whereabouts, nor where the vicar might have put it for safekeeping. Hopkins' men had seized the vicar and now the Witchfinder ordered them to hold him until his return, when he would personally ensure the vicar confessed to being a witch, as he stood accused by his village; and he would reveal where he had hidden the book, Kat's Grimoire. When asked where he was going the Witchfinder General replied:

"To Northampton to apprehend two witches and their travelling companion Tom Cobbold who, he had remembered, was the son of a woman he sent to trial as a witch. She had been lucky, the Magistrate found her not guilty. Her son would not be so fortunate."

14
NASEBY

We had finished the last of the food Madeleine had put into the saddlebags and there was no ale left. The horses were tiring but it could not be far to Northampton. A milestone confirmed this and we now had to decide if we could continue to Naseby before nightfall. I knew the battle, if it was to happen, would begin the following morning. I really wanted to find Gubbins before the battle. That set me thinking again about how the Time Thing worked. When I arrived at the battle the last time I had travelled with Captain Dagger, (yes, the same Captain Dagger we had left looking for his horse).

That time we were at an inn in Naseby with a Royalist patrol when a load of Roundheads appeared and I had left Captain Dagger in a sword fight with one. I reached the battlefield and found Nathaniel, Gabriel's brother, who took me to Gabriel himself. This time it had to be different. There had to be a Time Shift, I was sure, because here I was riding with Kat and Tom Cobbold.

The decision whether we continued to Naseby was made for us by the presence of Roundheads everywhere in Northampton. The air was mild and we rode without our musketeer jackets, drawing little attention since everywhere was bustling with the news that Oliver Cromwell had arrived, joined a Council of War and was to stay the night at nearby Hazelrigg House. We skirted around Northampton and set out on the road to Naseby.

As we neared the village I thought it best if we stayed out of the centre in case we encountered the conflict between the Cavalier and Roundhead patrols. I did not want to encounter Captain Dagger again, if indeed he was there and had not ridden for Chinnor and Oxford. We rode north again. I needed to find Nathaniel first because I was sure Gabriel would, as before, be fighting with the Forlorn Hope. Nathaniel would know how to get me to Gubbins. I also knew the Royalists were on the north side of Naseby field where, in history, the battle took place. I thought back to when I was here before and became locked into my own battle with a Time Violator. That is not going to happen this time, I told myself.

Well, what happens next, when I tell you, you will not believe. We stumbled into the Royalist's 'whores' camp. You can imagine how we felt. Now we were in the Royalist area and the evening was getting cooler we had put on our jackets, looking like proper Musketeers.

There were hundreds of women, some young and pretty, some like ancient hags. There was cooking everywhere, enough to feed the army, so to speak. Some women, taking us for boys, shouted lewd invitations to us and we just smiled back. I looked for someone who might be in charge, someone who could tell me where we would find the main Royalist army camp. Tom Cobbold got down from his horse and walked over to a bucolic looking woman stirring a big pot over a makeshift fire. She wore a low cut bodice dress with a voluminous skirt. Her boobs were enormous. Tom was starting to enquire where we might find the main army troops when there was a big commotion on the edge of the camp.

Suddenly there were several riders coming towards us, like charging cavalry. Kat swung a look in my direction; Tom was reaching for his pistols. I reached into the saddlebag and found my loaded flintlock. The women were scattering, screaming as they ran and the horses thundered towards us. I could not take my eyes off the two leading riders. One was Matthew Hopkins, the Witchfinder General. The other was Jac.

***

Gabriel Gubbins sensed Klaudia was near. He was camped with the New Model Army south of Naseby. News had arrived that Oliver Cromwell was in Northampton and this very afternoon the Roundheads had been pursuing the Cavaliers. Cromwell's son-in-law, Commissary General Henry Ireton attacked a Royalist outpost at Naseby. The Roundheads were close to the King's army and everyone said the King would have to do battle or retreat with the Roundheads close behind.

The Voices were no help to Gubbins. He had called to them but there was no answer. Where were the Lords Temporal? Why had they not allowed Klaudia to come to him when he called? Was it they who were in control or, perhaps, it was the Time Masters who were preventing her from finding him? Here, history was repeating itself for him and yet it was all slightly different. He wondered why Somerset had not used her powers to reach him. Maybe she had, when the strange girl had appeared with the message. He did not have a chance to ask her more before she disappeared as quickly as she had come.

As a Traveller, Gubbins knew Klaudia had immense power but he also knew she had barely learned how to control it. She had managed to overcome a Time Violator, a daemon sent by the Time Masters to assassinate King Charles 1 and Oliver Cromwell. Would that part of history repeat itself the second time around? He had no way of telling. There was a noise outside the tent, then a whisper.

"Gabriel, come quietly, bring your pistols and sword. Your Somerset is in the Royalist whores' camp. I have horses ready." Gubbins stepped out of the tent to find his brother, Nathaniel, waiting with two horses saddled.

"She and others have been hunted by a witchfinder and he has them trapped in the whores' camp. We must ride fast if we are to save her. I hear this witchfinder is vicious and his men greedy for money and power. Somerset has been here before. She knows the outcome of the battle and could be an influence on the course taken by the generals. It could change history." The two young men had mounted up and were riding for the whores' camp.

I had time only to fire one shot which I aimed at the Witchfinder General. I did not aim to kill him. Klaudia Cay doesn't go around killing people. The bullet went straight past his ear and he pulled his horse up sharply, as did the other riders, Roundhead soldiers by the look of them.

Jac had leapt from her horse and was running towards me, shouting abuse. There was no time to load a pistol. I drew my sword. It rested easily in my hand. It felt natural. I could see Tom Cobbold was fighting two Roundheads and Kat came running to help me with Jac.

What happened next was very, very frightening. Jac's whole body was changing. First it was her face. It began to morph. It was becoming a death mask, like the Time Violator I had fought before. The mouth opened and a forked tongue came out, reaching towards me. Her body was changing as well. What did my dad call it? Metamorphosis. She was turning into a man. The death mask changed again and now she was becoming a Roundhead, fierce in the attack. No longer Jac, this man she had become seemed massively strong. He did not know or care who I was. A teenage girl. I was the enemy to be killed. I should have realised what was happening. It was my nightmare. Now it was real. I had never fought anyone like this before.

He struck the first blow. I should have known it was coming, with everything Gabriel Gubbins had taught me. Where was Gubbins? Why was he not here? I tried to use my Time Power to force the Roundhead back but it was not like before when I drove the Time Violator to Oblivion. This was not working. It was then I caught sight of Gabriel Gubbins and his brother, Nathaniel, running out of the woods.

My Gubbins had come. Too late. I felt the searing pain in my side. In that moment I had not fixed my eyes on my adversary, to catch the flicker in his eyes and sense where his next lunge would be. I was angry at myself and it was days since I had had my last pill. I parried the next blow and found a split second between life and death. I saw Tom Cobbold go down, two Roundheads on him like a rash. Kat was behind me, back to back, my rear guard, and I heard the clash of steel on steel as she fought for her life. I'm sorry Kat, I made you a promise to get you home.

The sword in my hand seemed now to have a life of its own. I thrust forward and upward. The Roundhead's leather jacket was open at the front, offering no protection. He wore no breast plate of armour. I sliced easily through the doublet and his white shirt. A crimson line appeared. He had a questioning look on his face, as if he did not understand what had happened. I lunged forward again, sensing Kat had pushed her opponent backwards too.

I let out a scream as my anger rose. They were not going to win, I would see to that. I spun right round and in that moment caught sight of Kat falling to the ground. I screamed again as I turned and my sword sliced across the Roundhead's stomach, deep and fatal.

He staggered back for a moment, dropping his sword as he held his belly, his guts beginning to spill out into his hand. I saw Gabriel Gubbins running towards me. Too late. The Roundhead's face morphed back into the death mask of a Time Violator. My pain was intense, stabbing. I clutched my side and I could see the blood flowing as the light faded with my life force.

Gabriel and Nathaniel Gubbins knew they were too late as they ran from the woods towards the sword fight. They saw Somerset, Klaudia Cay, spin round to bring the full force of her sword across the belly of a Roundhead before her. A move Gabriel remembered teaching her, to gain the most power and effective slice of the honed sword edge.

Behind her, on the ground and held with the tip of a sword at her throat was a girl dressed as a boy, a young Musketeer, her blond hair streaked with the red of her own blood. A young man lay nearby. Gabriel Gubbins could not tell if he was dead or knocked unconscious with the butt of the musket in the hands of a Roundhead who stood over him. Gubbins and Nathaniel slowed their pace to a walk. At that moment Somerset seemed to be falling, her sword dropped, a bloodied hand holding her side. Then she simply disappeared.

The Roundhead she had slain was motionless for a moment, standing with his guts in his hand, then he sank to his knees as his body changed. The face was the face of death. Fleetingly he became a girl who Gubbins knew. Then there was just a pile of clothes that in an instant turned to dust. Nathaniel put a hand on his brother's arm.

"Let me deal with them, brother, contain your anger. These people know not who we are." Nathaniel stepped towards the man with the tall hat who seemed to be presiding over the other men and who indeed said:

"Enough, I want them alive, to go to trial as witches. Bind their wounds and then bring them to me." Matthew Hopkins gave the command. Gabriel Gubbins had a strong sense of what had occurred and he knew this had all the marks of a Time Master's work.

Somerset was gone, he knew not where. He cursed for being too late. He did not recognise the blond girl or the young fellow who was being pulled groggily to his feet, holding his bruised head. He did, though, recognise the girl with the jet black hair, the piercings and tattoos, standing next to the man who was obviously the leader of this troop. The same girl he had seen reduced to ashes a moment before. How could that be? He knew her name was Jac. There was the devil's work afoot. He had seen Jac before, in another time, when Somerset had travelled and ridden with him. He knew Jac was a Follower and able to travel through time, almost at will. Her powers were well developed, more so than Somerset's. It explained a lot, how Klaudia came to be in 1645 but had not arrived at his calling. Someone else was in control. He wondered if Jac would recognise him too.

"How can I help you, gentlemen?" Matthew Hopkins stared at Gabriel and Nathaniel.

"We heard gunfire and came to find the cause." Nathaniel said.

"And what, pray, are you doing near the Royalist's whores camp? Should you not be with the New Model Army?"

"We are acting as scouts for Commissary General, General Henry Ireton, looking for Royalist patrols. And you sir, what is your business in these parts?" Nathaniel challenged.

"I am Matthew Hopkins, Witchfinder General, and I am here to apprehend these witches, to return them to Bury St Edmunds for trial. Found guilty they will be hanged by the neck as an example of the fate of those who practice maleficium. Witness the ones who disappeared. You have seen, with your own eyes, witchcraft being manifest this day." Gubbins felt the icy look of the Witchfinder upon him.

"There is another we seek, perhaps you know of him," Hopkins said, "the witches call him Gabriel Gubbins. Do you know that name?" Nathaniel cut in before Gubbins could answer.

"We know of no one by that name sir, there are thousands of troops here with the army. But if we were to come across such a name we would be pleased to inform you. How can we reach you in the event?"

"As I say, I will return to Brandeston from whence

these witches came, and then to Bury. We will find the truth about the witches' manifestations and an explanation of the disappearance of the one we know to have travelled from some future time. She, the witch dressed as a boy, goes by the name Klaudia Cay."

"Then if we hear of this Gubbins or of the witch we will send word to you, sir," Nathaniel gave a little mock bow, "and may God go with you. We will take our leave." Nathaniel motioned to Gabriel who had a sense of relief that Jac appeared not to recognise him; or if she did she said nothing to the witchfinder. He had an urge to take down the man but he realised the forces were many and another sense told him they were not all human. Another day, he thought, when we discover what has happened to Somerset, we will approach the demise of this charlatan with relish and a plan. For now we will return to our stations, for this is the eve of the Battle of Naseby.

PART TWO

15
MISSING PERSONS

"The search continues for two missing teenagers." The TV newsreader announced on the BBC Six o'clock News.

"Hungarian-born Katalin Danko and her friend, Jacqueline Hamilton-Smith, disappeared after a Halloween party at the Oxfordshire residence of John and Caroline Cay. The Cays, who own the Manor Farm Estate near the Oxfordshire village of Little Haseley, are believed to have made a fortune from a dot com travel company and computers for schools. They are helping Thames Valley Police with their enquiries. All that is known so far is that the missing teenagers, and the Cay's daughter Klaudia, had been playing Halloween games in a secret passage that links the Cay's sixteenth century farmhouse with a nearby chapel.

"Two other teenagers at the party, Alice Penfold from Oxford and Brandi Maddison, the daughter of American film director Brad Maddison Jnr. are also assisting the police. We will have more news of this breaking story later in the programme." The newsreader moved on to other less dramatic stories of the day.

"It makes us all sound like rich bitches and like it's something we did." Bran said as I turned down the sound on the remote. There was me, Bran and Slick Alice in the Tapestry Room where my parents had told us to stay, with the media clamouring at the gates to our farm estate.

"And to say Kat and Jac are friends, well, where did that come from?" Slick Alice stared out of the window, out of the line of sight of the telescopic lenses of the Paparazzi.

"You read about these things, you never think one day it might happen to you." I said. "The problem is we can't tell them anything. No one is going to believe us. They will think we're making it up and then it gets worse. Next thing they'll be looking for bodies in the cellar, or the secret passage."

Let me tell you what happened. I had found myself back in the chapel, next to the font, with Bran and Slick Alice. The party was still going on because only a few minutes had passed since I had travelled back to 1645 and returned. During those minutes though, Scary Mary had walked back to the party saying it was best if she was talking to people while I travelled, 'to keep them occupied.'

Now of course Slick Alice and Bran know all about the Time Thing, from when I travelled before, and together with Kat we are all sworn to secrecy. I couldn't tell them what had happened to her. I was sure Jac was OK as she always is and she was up to no good as usual. We had gone back to the party and found Scary Mary. She looked very concerned and said she would talk to Shelley and my parents. I wondered why she would talk to my parents but for the moment we left it at that. The party broke up. Kat was supposed to have stayed on a sleepover. The following morning my mum asked where she was. I lied. I told her she had decided to go home with Bran because she wanted to talk to Bran's dad about doing film studies. Bad move. Because when you tell one lie you almost invariably have to tell more and so things go from bad to really bad to even worse.

No one really took much notice when Kat and Jac didn't turn up for school. Until teachers rang parents. Parents rang parents. Parents asked us where they were. We were mystified, we said. Maybe they ran away together we joked. It got serious. The police were called. There was the nice Detective Inspector Brooks who turned up with a lady detective. Both of them were fit. It was like being in the television series Midsomer Murders. They film that a lot around Oxfordshire and our villages.

Then it gets really serious. It's on the national news, the BBC and ITV. Then this big hunt starts. They've got sniffer dogs down by the Oxfordshire canal and along the Isis River, the part of the Thames near Bran's home. They took it very seriously when Bran told them Kat had gone home to her place and decided to go for a walk along the river and didn't come back. Bran's dad is an American film director but her mum is English and most of the time they live in England. Bran's as English as I am. I had never realised Kat was Hungarian. She's always been, well, just Kat. She came to England when she was only two-years old. Her parents are professors at Reading University.

What can I tell you about Slick Alice? Her family is not rich or anything. Her dad is a writer. He writes mystery novels and thriller scripts. The police were very interested in that. Jac's parents, the Hamilton-Smiths, were making no comment. We always thought Jac came from an underprivileged background, with all her problems when she arrived at our school. It turns out her family is mega-rich but no one seems to know how they made their money. So I suppose it does seem as if we are rich bitches but it's not like we go around shouting about it. Now we were in big trouble.

It was like everyone was under investigation and there was absolutely nothing I could say or do. I was hoping Scary Mary and Shelley would come up with a plan. The trouble was, with everything going on, I did not get to see Mary until the following weekend when I had a dressage lesson booked. It was the worst week ever, with all the police and media thing. I am back on my medication because the ADHD really kicked in again. I hate my parents. They are making my life hell. Everyone is blaming them for what happened and they are blaming me, Bran and Slick Alice.

I am also very confused because I did not know how I got home from 1645. I had a really bad pain in my side and tummy again and I could not explain exactly what had happened in the sword fight with the Roundhead. I remembered seeing Gabriel Gubbins then it all went blank and I thought I was dying.

Then I remembered something. A Time Princess has so many lives. A bit like the cat's said to have nine but no one knows how many lives a Traveller has. Maybe that was it. I had used one up. I had the pain but there was no cut or bruise or anything. I could not explain it. I was more worried about Kat. What had happened to her? We still had to go into school that week and usually I would take the bus but mum decided it was for the best if she dropped me off and collected me. The other girls' parents were doing the same. The week did seem to drag on. I have trouble concentrating at school. This was worse than usual. Everything in lessons was boring, with all the things going on around us. Police at the school. Interviews with the Head Mistress about Kat and Jac. Where they liked to go, who they had as friends outside school. I thought about telling the teachers that Kat and Jac were definitely not friends but for once I decided to keep my mouth shut.

I did try to call Shelley, my old swimming coach, but she was not answering her 'phone. I was feeling guilty. Here I was, back at school, all this going on around us and nothing I could do was bringing Kat back. In our history class, Mr Payne was still going on about King Charles 1 and the Levellers and that made me want to scream.

"What about the witchfinder and the witch hunts?" I actually shouted at one point in the lesson. Everything went quiet and all the class turned to look at me.

"We've already touched on witch-hunting, Klaudia, why do you want to go back on that?" Mr. Payne asked.

"Was it true that Matthew Hopkins earned a fortune from witch-hunting?" I asked.

"Well, I can see you were paying attention in at least one lesson, Klaudia Cay. There has always been some debate about whether Hopkins did what he did to make money or out of some religious fervour. We do know in one instance he charged, I believe it was Stowmarket, twenty three pounds for a witch-hunt in the town, which in today money would buy you a nice small car. But so little is known about Matthew Hopkins, apart from being the most prolific witch hunter in English history, much is speculation. What we do know is the term witch-hunt has been passed down to the modern day, thought now it has taken on another meaning. Anything thought to undermine today's society and present day values can lead to a 'witch-hunt' to find the culprits. So that is one legacy Hopkins left behind him. Now, we digress, the Levellers..." Mr. Payne was back to the Smart Board and continued the lesson...

After school I went for fencing lessons with Antonia, my fencing teacher. She said I must have been practicing and that I had made a big improvement to my technique. Little did she know. But it was not the same without Kat.

That night, when I got home, I did my pony, feeding him and putting a rug on him and then I went to the chapel. I put my hands on the rim of the font and I though hard about Kat and where she might be. I was sure she would be alright. She's tough, my mate. I thought about Gabriel Gubbins and Naseby. He would be looking for me. I tried to summon my powers but nothing came of it.

I went back to the house and we had supper. The news was on TV and the hunt for Kat and Jac was no longer the main story. It was all about a load of spies who had been secretly hacking into government computers for years. One of them was a famous politician and no one could believe he was a spy.

"Another witch hunt," my dad said. How ironic. In fact, that was about all that was said over supper. Mum wasn't making any conversation and I said I wanted to go to my room because I was tired and the teachers had been really hard on us all day. Going on about always telling parents where we were going and who we were seeing. Now I know that's a good thing but what they did not know was there are Travellers and some things just can't be explained. I cried myself to sleep with worry that night. When I woke up I knew one thing.

I had to go back and rescue Kat and put an end to Jac's devious time tricks. I would be taking on the might of the Witchfinder General and his men. I would find Gabriel Gubbins and together we would do it. Gubbins and me. We were winners. There had to be a way.

So, that weekend we were grounded in that we were not allowed to go into Oxford and meet at McDees or Costa. But my parents suggested to Slick Alice's and Bran's parents it would be alright if they came over to our place where they could at least get away from the Paparazzi. All week the photographers had been waiting outside school until we came out and they took lots of pictures as we got into the cars with our mums.

My dad said our security would keep them out of our estate and we could talk about what happened and what to do. A bit like a Council of War, I thought. First though, I had a dressage lesson booked with Scary Mary early on Saturday morning. She kept a stiff face while my dad was around watching my lesson. My horse, Solo, never went better for me and Mary said we were ready to compete in the championships. I had to admit to myself I was really liking the dressage because I suddenly discovered how much control I had, as if Solo and I were one entity, doing the movements in complete harmony. I also discovered how clever and good he was.

Scary Mary shouted a bit as usual but I could sense she was pretty pleased with how it was going. Dad had gone back to the house but mum had come out and Mary walked over to her and took her to one side, talking quietly (for a change). That worried me. I walked Solo around the arena while they talked for quite a while and then mum came over and said she was taking Beth, my little sister, shopping and that Mary would stay on to talk me through the tests we would need to do to prepare for the next stage in the championships. Mum said she would be back with lunch for Alice, Bran and their parents. I pulled a face. I hadn't realised their parents were coming too. Then mum gave me her list of orders on what to do on the yard. Mixing feed and filling hay nets for the horses, sweeping up, bringing the horses in, and picking out their hooves. And she asked me if I had taken my pills that morning. I lied. I said yes. It's just that I forget to do things. Part of the attention deficit disorder, they tell me. I thought OK. I will take the pills later.

Now I needed to talk to Mary and tell her what happened, to see what we had to do to get Kat back home. I'm sure that's why Mary had stayed on. She listened carefully as I told her the whole story and by the end of it she looked really very worried.

"This is the work of a Time Master," she said, "and Jac's powers have developed faster than any of us could imagine. The Lords Temporal allowed Gabriel Gubbins to travel back to 1645, to find you and help you get home but the Time Master intervened and sent him straight to the march to Naseby. This much I know.

"Now we have to find a way to sort out the mess. Kat and Jac are missing persons. The police are suggesting foul play and anyone in any way connected, friends, family, teachers, me, you, are suspects. Then there are the Paparazzi who are like terriers. They won't let go until they have a sensational story that sells a whole lot more newspapers. The Lords Temporal are fully aware of all that has happened."

"Then why don't they let me use my power. Last time I travelled I had power. Others, like Madeleine (I had told Mary about her) seem to be able to travel at will and I'm stuck on the back of a horse riding for days to get to Naseby." I was feeling quite angry about this.

"You have to be patient, Klaudia. The Lords have concerns about your abilities because of your, well, let's call it your 'condition'. They don't want to allow a situation where any harm could come to you." I almost laughed at this, thinking about all the scrapes and near misses I had been in.

"Then what about the sword fight with the Roundhead? He wasn't real you know, he was a Time Violator, I am sure. And that was the day before the Battle of Naseby. Last time I was there I fought a Time Violator on the battlefield and I lost. What has happened? Has history changed? Is there a battle?"

"The Battle of Naseby remains in history, the deciding moment in the English Civil War. For you, something has changed. We must see how best we can take all that has happened and find a way to bring Kat, and Jac, home. To do this the Lords have demanded a Quorum. That is, we gather at least the minimum number of Travellers in one place. Each one has to be descended from the Royal Family in the House of Time. There are three such Travellers, each a Time Princess, like yourself and this weekend we will form the Quorum."

"Who are they, do I know them?" I asked.

"You know all of them, but you must wait until the Quorum is formed. Then all will be revealed." I was really frustrated by that but there was not much I could do. Mary said she would tell my mum we needed another lesson tomorrow, on the Sunday, and then she would tell me more. So I had to be patient. That is not easy, I can tell you. Mary walked over to her car.

"I will see you tomorrow, Klaudia. For now it is best that you and the other girls keep to your story. Kat disappeared when she went for a walk near Bran's home. Jac you know nothing about. None of us can tell the truth, because no one will believe it." It was the first time I had been told by a teacher it was OK to lie. I knew, though, there was no choice and it was better this way, for now. Who would believe there were time travellers and witches living in Oxford and disappearing back to 1645? As Mary drove off I turned back to the yard and started the chores I had been given, trying to remember what mum said I needed to do.

16
THE BATTLE OF NASEBY

At first, Gabriel Gubbins found it strange that he had left his brother, Nathaniel, standing in the chapel near their home in 1647. Now he was here with him two years earlier in 1645, here as the New Model Army gathered its forces to face King Charles 1 and the Cavaliers. There was little time though to dwell on this. Gubbins had fleetingly seen Klaudia, Somerset, as she was to him. Some trick of time had occurred and there was no more he could do for now except prepare for battle. He was sure Somerset would not appear again. Everything was slightly different from the last time he was here. Nathaniel, in his role as an Intelligencer, had returned to the Royalist army.

Morning had broken on the 14th June 1645 to reveal a heavy fog descended on Naseby and neither army could see each other. Gubbins was following orders along with the others in The Forlorn Hope of Musketeers, priming their weapons in readiness for battle.

Gubbins heard no voices to tell him of the whereabouts of Somerset. She had disappeared before his eyes. So near, so close. He could only hope the Lords Temporal had a plan to counter the Time Master who was controlling the destinies of so many. It was a Time Master, Gubbins was sure, who had brought him back here, to the Battle of Naseby where he had been shot. What would happen this time? He had no answer but to do battle and await his fate. He lived in the hope that he would survive to help Somerset. He had come to realise that whatever trouble she was in, it had more than something to do with the Witchfinder General. It was strange that Jac, whom he knew from when he and Somerset had fought her before, had said nothing when he and Nathaniel had confronted the witchfinder. She had appeared, or pretended, not to know Gubbins. He could find no reason for this.

General Fairfax had considered occupying the northern slopes of Naseby Ridge, until Oliver Cromwell pointed out the position was too strong. The Royalists would not fight them there, he said. As the mists began to clear, Fairfax moved the army back a little and the Forlorn Hope of Musketeers was ordered to take up positions. Gubbins eased forward with them, musket at the ready, as the two armies claimed their positions and gathered their battle formations.

***

I was not happy. My parents had set a trap by asking Slick Alice and Bran's parents to come with them. It turned out Jac's parents, the Hamilton-Smiths and Kat's parents had also been invited but had declined. It seemed we were being blamed for Kat and Jac's disappearance, since it all happened around our Halloween party. It was unusual because it was my dad who started on me. Usually it's mum but she sat very tight-lipped and said nothing.

We were questioned again about the party and how we came to know about the secret passage. I did not know how they had found out about it and I was angry they knew and worse, they had taken this as some sort of game we played on Halloween. How stupid is that?

Anyway, it was Bran who had come up with the best story and we all stuck to it. She told them that a chauffeur-driven car had arrived for Jac and she had offered to give Kat and Bran a lift to Bran's house. This was a cool idea because Kat and Bran were supposed to be on a sleepover but this fitted with her wanting to go to meet Bran's dad and talk about a film course.

Bran said Jac dropped them off and, they thought, went off in the chauffeur-driven car. Kat and Bran had gone into the house and Bran's parents were out, not expecting Bran to come home. Then, she said, Kat had decided she wanted to be alone for a bit and had gone for a walk. She did not return. I have to admit, Bran can make up a pretty good story.

Of course, the Hamilton-Smiths were not there so there was no one to confirm if they had sent a car to collect Jac. For now at least. Somehow, Bran knew a lot more about Jac than we did. Later she told me she had seen Jac in Oxford one day, getting into a limo with blacked out windows. She had recognised Jac's mum from last term when Jac had been causing big problems and her mum had come to see the Head Mistress.

Now I have seen enough Midsomer Murder mysteries to know the police will get to the truth. But it seemed for now that Bran's story was standing up. I was hoping Scary Mary had a plan and we could get all this sorted.

It was lunchtime and mum had bought sandwiches for everyone and poured some drinks for the parents. We girls sneaked some beers upstairs to the Tapestry

Room and I found my iPad. We looked up Matthew Hopkins, Witchfinder General on Wiki.

Now this is scary. There was a list of names of people accused of being witches. I stared at the names. Anne Wright and Anne Leech were among them. Now I was really frightened for Kat. There was not much else. Matthew Hopkins' early life was a bit of a mystery. It did not seem as if it would tell us much we didn't already know until Slick Alice found a reference to a book. Hopkins was, it was said, in possession of a book he had cleverly cheated out of the hands of the Devil himself. It was a book that would help him in his witchhunting.

We looked at each other and we didn't need to say anything because we were all thinking the same thing. What if the book was really Kat's Grimoire? I had told them Hopkins was after her book. Were these books one and the same? We looked up the Battle of Naseby and it all said much the same as we had done in our history lesson.

Bran and Slick Alice went home with their parents. I had forgotten to take my pills and I felt like a fit was coming on. So I went to lock myself in my room. George, my brother, came in.

"You're doing it again, aren't you?"

"Doing what?" I asked.

"The time travel stuff." He said, with a knowing look on his face.

"I don't know what you're talking about. Leave me alone. I want to sleep."

"Not until you tell me."

"Tell you what?"

"How you came to have these?" I stared in disbelief. He was aiming my two flintlock pistols from 1645 straight at me. They had been in my belt when I fought the Roundhead.

"George, put them down, they're loaded, they could go off."

"Not until you tell me how you do it. I saw you. You went to the chapel during the party, with your mates, and you stood by the font. Then, you just disappeared. When you came back you've got two pistols. Where did you go?"

"It is none of your business. Give me the pistols."

"I'm making it my business." He mimicked some movie actor voice.

"George, it's not a game. This is serious."

"It must be, the way the police and the newspapers are all over us." I knew then it was George who had told on us, about the secret passage. He must have followed and spied on us. How else would he know? Maybe he told the police and the press a load of stuff. Maybe they were paying him. I did not know what to do. Just at that moment we heard someone coming up the stairs. I surprised George by grabbing the guns and pushing them under the mattress on my bed.

"I might throw a fit and tell everyone about you and that girl Caz and what you were both doing at the party." I challenged as mum walked in.

"Mum, George is doing it again. I am trying to get some space in my room and George wants to know how I can be a time traveller. How stupid is that?" Mum looked at me in a funny way and then said quietly, but firmly:

"George, Klaudia has not taken her pills today so I would be a little careful if I were you." I wondered how she knew I had forgotten to take the pills. Mum turned to me again.

"Alright Klaudia, whatever you are thinking of doing I expect you to go and do your pony and feed the horses before we have dinner. No argument." Secretly, I was glad to go back to the yard and do the horses early. I began thinking about what the Quorum would do. When I came in the news was on the TV. It was claimed that Kat and Jac had been seen boarding a train in London, bound for the Channel Tunnel and France. They were accompanied by two young men, described as eastern European-looking. Questions were being asked. Perhaps they had been kidnapped. For what purpose?

Now I knew that was a load of rubbish but selfishly I thought at least it would keep the police occupied for a while. Then Kat's parents appeared on the news. Kat's mum with tears streaming down her face, appealing to anyone who could help find Kat and bring her home safely. What could I do? I felt guilty. I was determined I would bring her back from 1645 but I could not do that on my own. Then I got a text message. It was Gabriel Gubbins. How does he do that?

"Somerset, I saw you but for a moment, fighting the spectre of a Roundhead. It was one sent to destroy you. I feel you are safe and I call you once again to return. The Battle of Naseby begins but I will survive to be with you. Together we shall win!" Gubbins.

So Gubbins had called me again. I tried texting back but I knew it was no use. I also knew if I was to travel again I had to be allowed by my Patron, or Patrons now, plural, as Scary Mary had told me. I wanted tomorrow to come. Who was my third Patron? I could not guess.

I went to my room after dinner, played some games, downloaded from iTunes, got bored, tried to sleep. But I kept seeing the Roundhead I had fought and even when I did get to sleep the nightmare came back. This time I did not wake up screaming. I woke up with one thing on my mind. To put an end to the witch hunts and bring down Matthew Hopkins.

***

King Charles 1 was in shining gilt armour and riding a Flemish horse. As the mists cleared over Naseby his army, their colours flying and their own gleaming armour reflecting the sun, marched across the New Model Army's front. The King had sent out the Royal Scoutmaster, Sir Francis Ruce, to find the Roundhead army but he had returned saying he'd had no sight of it. Prince Rupert rode ahead and came back with news he had seen Parliamentarian cavalry. He told the King he would secure Naseby Ridge. The King, persuaded by his grooms and courtiers to engage battle, chose the password for the day: Queen Mary. Word was passed throughout the Royalist army and so they took up their positions.

On the right wing, under the command of Prince Rupert and Prince Maurice were 3000 cavalry, their horses snorting and fighting to be in the charge. In the centre, under Colonel Howard, was the 'Northern Horse,' cavalry who had come from the North of England to join the fight. The King led his own command of a small reserve. The Royalist army was impressive, their bright uniforms spreading colour across the ground known as Broad Moor as they moved to their positions. They numbered about 7,400 men.

Oliver Cromwell and the Roundheads had 13,500. Nearly twice as many men. General Fairfax was commanding the Roundhead army and he positioned the men on Naseby Ridge before Prince Rupert could get there. Many men were hidden behind the ridge, on the reverse slope. Gabriel Gubbins marched out with the Forlorn Hope of 300 Musketeers to form the first line of defence. The ground shook as Prince Rupert and Prince Maurice began the attack, riding their horses slowly and in very stately fashion at first, then suddenly gathering speed and thundering down a slope, under fire from Roundhead dragoons hidden in Sulby Hedges on their right. Still they charged towards the Roundheads who had moved forward to meet them over the crest of the hill. There was a crescendo of gunfire from muskets and Carabines, shouts and screams, the heavy snorting of horses and the pounding of hooves. Gabriel Gubbins had only one shot at the awesome sight of four thousand horses charging towards him. Then he felt the searing heat and pain engulf his body as a pistol bullet creased his chest, splitting bone where it entered his shoulder and passed to exit through his back. He felt he was dying with the pain that followed, his head swirling, he started to fall, the light in his eyes fading to a sudden blinding flash of a cavalry sword barely missing slicing his face in two. His last thought at this moment was of Somerset, Klaudia, and how he had failed her.

***

When I woke up on Sunday morning I could hear mum in the kitchen, banging about with pots and pans. I heard dad's voice, saying he was taking the quad and going to fix the fence on the far side of the farm, where journalists had broken through and got nearly all the way to the house. They had been stopped by the policeman assigned to us and 'the case of the missing teenagers.' I dressed and came downstairs. Mum said she would have bacon and eggs ready for dad when he came back. I sat down and had cereal, then the bacon and eggs.

After breakfast I went over to the stables and saddled Solo, my horse, ready to for when Scary Mary arrived to give me my dressage lesson. Dad went past on the quad. I knew mum wouldn't be long so I started working Solo in the arena, taking him through a dressage test I would have to do for the championships.

As I was riding around, trying to remember the test, my heart leapt. Standing at the end of the arena was Shelley, my old swimming coach. She was also my old Patron, the one who could sponsor me to time travel. Then Scary Mary arrived as well. Mary started the dressage lesson and while I was riding Mum appeared. Mary called us all to the middle of the arena.

"I have talked with the Lords Temporal," she said, "and they have passed sanction. This means you can Travel, Klaudia." I was standing in front of her, Shelley and my mum, doing my cod act, my mouth opening and closing but nothing coming out. What was weird was that Mary was saying this in front of mum. I had never been able to tell her about the time travelling and here was Mary talking about me travelling again.

"I can see you're puzzled by this, Klaudia, you have been in a quandary for a long time. Whether to tell your mother about the Travelling. You were scared she would not believe you. Today, we have a Quorum. Me, Shelley, your mum and you. We are each of us Travellers and Time Princesses. Your mother has known about you travelling all along but could not tell you. She is your mother but she is also a Princess of The House of Time and must obey the rules of the Lords Temporal. The situation with Kat, and Jac for that matter, cannot be allowed to continue. We needed a Quorum to end it and at this point in time we are the only ones who can work together with you, to put a stop to the doings of Matthew Hopkins."

"Remember, when you were at the Battle of Naseby, the first time you travelled," Shelley cut in, "you were defeated by the Time Violator? He and his Time Master put you into a Time Slip. You were, literally, stuck in time. You could see time passing and history unfolding but there was nothing you could do. Listen carefully, when you time travel you are using different astral planes. Much in the same way witches do. We are going to work with the Lords Temporal to create a parallel astral plane to send you back to 1645, taking you from the time you were in the Time Slip. That way it will have no effect on time itself, or change history. What it will do is allow you to join Gabriel Gubbins, find Kat and campaign for the end of witch hunting. Together we will all work to bring you home. There is some powerful force that has prevented us from bringing Kat back with you. Between us all we must overcome it and get you both home safely."

My cod had turned into a wet one, slapping me around the face so to speak. I had woken up this morning to a different world. My mum knew about me time travelling. She was a Time Princess too. We had a Quorum. There was something we could do to rescue Kat. Gabriel Gubbins must be alright. My head was in a spin.

***

Henry Ireton, a tall, dark lawyer from Nottinghamshire and the man who would marry Oliver Cromwell's daughter, led the Roundhead cavalry charge against Prince Rupert. He rode so fast and hard he went straight through the lines of charging Cavaliers. He was wounded in the thigh and face as Rupert and his men broke through the Roundheads' left wing, chasing them away from the battlefield. Ireton could do nothing to rally his men, while Rupert's kept riding until they came to the Roundheads' baggage train, a mile or so behind the Parliamentarians' line.

The Royalists on the battlefield were gaining ground, driving the Roundheads back. Until Oliver Cromwell and his 'Ironsides' led a charge through the Royalists' infantry and appeared in front of the King and his reserves on Dust Hill. The King moved to take part in the battle but his Scottish friend, the Earl of Carnwarth, grabbed the King's horse's bridle, swearing and shouting:

"Will you go upon your death?" The King's horse reared and turned and, with part of the reserve following, the King rode away from the battlefield.

Cromwell chose not to chase the King's Life Guards and instead charged back into the battle. The Roundhead Dragoons in Sulby Hedges had mounted their horses and joined the battle. The rest of Henry Ireton's men rallied as well. Outnumbered by two to one and surrounded by Roundheads, the Royalist infantry began to lay down their arms. Many tried to retreat. Only Prince Rupert's Bluecoats stood their ground to the last, cut down by Fairfax's Regiment of Foot and Lifeguard of Horse.

Prince Rupert himself, away from the battle, was wearing a red Montero cap, like one worn by the Roundhead's General Fairfax. At first the baggage train commander mistook him for the General but when told to surrender by Rupert he refused and his men aimed their muskets at the prince. He and his men turned and galloped away, back to the battle, only to find the Royalists defeated. All he could do was cover the retreat of the King.

Gabriel Gubbins lay still, lifeless looking, in a ditch. Already he had been stripped of his clothes, like many of the two hundred Roundheads and seven hundred Royalists lying dead around him. The living wounded screamed and howled for surgeons to attend them. Four to five thousand Royalists had been captured. The King had lost with the battle his infantry, his own baggage train with his private papers and his throne. Night fell on the Battle of Naseby and the air chilled, as did the hearts of the Royalist soldiers not wounded, as they were marched as prisoners to Market Harborough church.

Nathaniel Gubbins watched from the cover of Sulby Hedges at sunrise as Roundheads stripped clothes from

Cavalier bodies, taking rings from fingers and from purses the ample money Cavaliers carried.

"This one still breathes." One man shouted, as he stood over the motionless body of Gabriel Gubbins.

"Let us kill him then. Slice his guts so he bleeds to death on England's soil. Let today be a lesson to all who support the King, the Catholics and the Pope." He raised his sword to strike. Nathaniel Gubbins strode purposefully out of the hedges.

"Hold there, he is a parliamentarian, same as you and me."

"How know you of this?"

"He is my brother, a Musketeer of the Forlorn Hope, the bravest of men."

"Then we be right sorry for our mistake. He has no clothes and lies among Royalists."

"An easy mistake to make, let us take him to a surgeon's tent where they can tend his wounds."

"Aye, he be lucky, the cold of the night stopped the flow of blood. Perhaps he will live." They lifted Gabriel who was gaining consciousness and moaning as they carried him to one of the hastily erected tents. The surgeon looked at the wounds and immediately used the Paré method of ointment, egg white, oil of roses and turpentine, applied to the bullet wounds front and back. He then bandaged them.

"I cannot be sure he will live," the surgeon said, "the poultice is his best hope and we pray the turpentine may stem the infection." He turned his attentions to the next man brought in. Gubbins could hear the surgeon's voice and that of his brother but it was in the distance as he drifted in and out of consciousness. He knew, as a Traveller, he might be fortunate and still have lives left.

He had survived the bullet wound when he was at Naseby the first time. He could not be sure though if time had changed the outcome and he feared the worst. He felt as if he was walking towards a bright, white light in the distance. He saw Somerset, Klaudia, standing there, waiting for him, a halo of light surrounding her, arms outstretched to greet him, like a lover waiting for the embrace.

Suddenly, the girl-woman who had given him the trout before the battle appeared. It was as if she sprinkled something over the wound. She said, simply, "go, Gabriel Gubbins and do what you have to do. Time is on your side." Then she vanished.

***

We were standing in the chapel. Me, mum, Scary Mary and Shelley. The Quorum. Mary had talked to the Lords Temporal again and they were in agreement. Gubbins had already Called me and I could return to 1645. Together we would find Kat and bring her home. No one mentioned Jac again. I think we were in silent agreement she would do her own thing, whatever we tried to do. I was sworn to keep away from trouble. I protested, saying it was not easy with a Civil War going on and people out to get you. Just be careful, mum said. I will I replied. And I will have Gabriel Gubbins watching over me, I was thinking. I would also have two flintlock pistols hidden in my belt, under a loose shirt. I had finished my dressage lesson and turned my horse out in the paddock. I used the excuse I needed the loo and raced back into the house, up to my bedroom, where I retrieved the pistols from under the mattress. I was sure I would pick up a sword somewhere. After all, I was going back to a battlefield. I also remembered I had the bag of money the witches had given me. Bribery can get you a long way in 1645. And I had a potion they had mixed. Until now I had not used it. I did not really know what it would do but I kept it to hand. Ready.

I had my hands on the rim of the font in the chapel and the water was rippling. A sign that any moment I would be gone. A Traveller through time. The worst part about time travelling is when the tingle becomes so intense it's painful, that, and not knowing if you will land exactly where you want. The best part is arriving safely, in the right place and at the right time. Once, I had landed in a gaol full of Roundheads and that was not good. I had to bribe my way out.

Mum gave me a kiss. She doesn't usually do that.

"Take care, Klaudia," she said with a tear in her eye. I did not get the chance to reply because in the next moment I was in the middle of the Royalist whores' camp, on the road to Leicester. There were sumpter horses and wagons carrying ale, in convoy with royal coaches and hundreds of women. Mistresses and wives of Royalist soldiers, whores, camp followers. Many of them were Welsh. It really was the wrong moment to arrive. They were fleeing from the Battle of Naseby, their husbands and lovers defeated and taken prisoner. Worse, the Roundheads had pursued them and a troop had caught up. Some women with money and jewels paid the soldiers not to kill them but many of those who could not pay were cruelly murdered or their cheeks and noses slashed by the sword. Even some of the wealthy women (you could tell them from their dress) were disfigured without mercy.

I reached for my money bag. Like most of rest of the women I was wearing a smock, stockings, a corset, a petticoat and a waistcoat. I had a partlet around my neck and a shawl draped over my shoulders. On my head I had a coif, a sort of lace cap. The colours were natural or brown and grey, some greens and blues. I had my pistols hidden under the shawl.

Of course I had no sword, only the pistols to defend myself but there were too many soldiers to use them. As one of them rode up to me I had that sinking feeling this could be nasty. I had one hand on a pistol, thinking if I could shoot the Roundhead off his horse I could make my escape by riding away from the troops. It was a desperate thought.

Then, I could not believe my eyes. Under the Roundhead helmet I could see a smiling Gabriel Gubbins. He extended a hand to me, firmly gripping mine as he swung me up onto the back of the horse, kicking the animal into a canter, then a gallop as we rode away from the scene of carnage on the road to Leicester. I half-expected to hear gunfire or the sound of pounding hooves behind us but the other troops paid little attention to a fleeing couple. They were more occupied with cutting down the screaming common women and cooks who were brandishing knives, threatening the soldiers. I found out later the Roundheads had mistaken the Welsh women's accents for Irish women, who would kill Protestants given the chance.

I could not hold back the tears. I was riding with Gabriel Gubbins. There was a time when I thought I would never see him again. But here we were. I realised

I had missed him terribly. We avoided the roads and tracks where fleeing Royalists were being chased by Roundheads. We crossed fields at speed, the poor horse blowing but keeping the pace until we were well beyond Naseby and in the area occupied by Roundheads.

No one challenged us when we did come across people. Gubbins wore the Roundhead clothes of a musketeer and I could pass as plainly Puritan. At last we stopped at an inn and Gabriel lifted me down from the horse, looking straight into my eyes. He pulled me to him and hugged me. It felt good to be in his arms.

"Ho, Somerset, a sight for the sore eyes of a wounded soldier."

"Where, where are you wounded?" I was very concerned, remembering Gubbins had been shot the first time we were in the Battle of Naseby.

"By some strange magik the wounds healed. My brother, Nathaniel, took me to a surgeon. Perhaps the ointment he applied did its work but barely a scar shows after a few hours. It is like witchcraft."

"It may be," I said, "that is why I am here. We have to get to Brandeston and find my friend, Kat. She is in great danger from the Witchfinder General."

"Oh yes, the Witchfinder. The cause of trials and tribulations across the lands of Suffolk and Norfolk, even Northamptonshire. I met him after you were fighting a spectre. The Witchfinder had that girl with him from your time."

"Jac!"

"Aye, 'twas her. But she seemed not to know me. She showed no recognition."

"She is evil and cannot be trusted. She would have

a reason to pretend not to know you. She is working with the Witchfinder General, hunting down poor women and accusing them of witchcraft. I think they have Kat." "There was a fair-skinned girl they took with them. She had fought like a fury but they overcame her, and a young man who dressed like a pirate."

"Tom Cobbold!"

"You know him? How came you to know him?" There was just a hint of jealousy in Gabriel's voice, I thought.

"I rode with him and Kat to try and reach you at the battle. He helped us in Brandeston, where the Witchfinder has a camp, torturing suspected witches."

"He was sore hurt but alive, this Tom Cobbold. They took him after Nathaniel and I spoke with the Witchfinder. He was looking for a Gabriel Gubbins. Nathaniel said if we were to come across such a person we would inform the Witchfinder of his whereabouts." Gubbins was smiling at this and I started to laugh.

"I see you have your same good spirits, Somerset. Come, we will take refreshment at the inn and make a plan to rescue your friend."

"How did you get here, Gabriel?" I suddenly wondered how it could be that I was walking up to an inn in 1645 with Gabriel Gubbins. The last time we were together was in 1647."

"I called you, Somerset, to come to 1647 because the King disappeared from Hampton Court, afeared of a Leveller plot to kill him. But the Voices told me you were in 1645 and I was allowed to travel back to find and help you. Some force separated us and I found myself with the Roundhead army, back at the Battle of Naseby." Gubbins related. A serving girl had brought out to us two tankards of ale, as we sat at a table outside the inn. It was a warm day and I was really very warm with all the clothes I was wearing. The innkeeper appeared, wanting to please the Roundhead soldier before him. He had brought a bucket of water for the horse.

"You have come from the battlefield?" He asked. "Would you like food?" He posed, before we could answer. He said he had some fine trout and there was a new dish that was becoming very popular, using the fish.

"Cooked with wine and stuffed with herbs?" Ventured Gabriel.

"Aye sir, you know of this dish?"

"A young woman gave me some before the Battle of Naseby.

"You fought in the battle, sir? You must be brave and you live to tell the tale. More ale, for you and your..." He looked at me, as if to say, and what are you two doing together?

Gubbins looked thoughtful for a moment.

"My cousin, from Somerset. She followed the army, to help cook."

"Ah, yes, of course." He gave me a 'knowing' look. "Will you partake of the fish?"

"Thank you, innkeeper but no. Just bring some bread, baken and cheese for now. Here, the payment for your trouble." Gubbins slipped him a silver coin and the man shuffled off, a smile on his face. Being so overpaid for his ale and food was something he was not used to.

"This girl, the one who brought you the trout before the battle. What did she look like?" I asked Gabriel.
I was beginning to get an idea who it was.

"Dark of complexion, eyes of brown, a strange accent, a fine figure with an ample bosom. A comely wench."

"Madeleine!" I uttered.

"I know not her name, for she disappeared as mysteriously as she came. I am sure though, she was a Traveller."

"It was Madeleine. Tom Cobbold's sister. She told me she had seen you." I was feeling strangely jealous again, especially when he said:

"A fine looking young woman, if ever I saw one." Let's leave it at that, I was thinking.

"Gabriel, we have to get to Brandeston. I can't ride like this, and don't ask me why but the Lords won't let me time travel there."

"The Voices say it is too dangerous. Each time you or I travel there is a Time Master working against the powers of good. It is how I came to Naseby and not Brandeston. We will find you clothes and we need fresh horses, one for each of us. I am sure the innkeeper can help us." The food arrived and Gubbins stabbed a piece of cheese with a knife he took from a sheath on his belt. He took a swig of ale, pushing the pewter tray of food towards me.

"Good cheese, have some." He said as he turned to the innkeeper.

"We will pay a handsome sum for good horses. Know you of any? I have heard many from around here were taken by the army when Oliver Cromwell came this way." The inn was on the road to Huntingdon and Cambridge.

"Not all, I have two good horses, but no cart for your cousin to drive."

"Worry not about a cart. What about a tailor's shoppe? Is there one nearby?"

"You are close to Kettering, a market town. There you will find shoppes and the market." The innkeeper accepted more silver coins from Gubbins for the horses, doing a deal for Gubbins' horse, which was one from the battlefield and had gone lame. We finished the food and ale. The inn had an outside latrine and I used this, taking the opportunity to remove the corset and petticoat to make it easier to ride the horse. I bundled everything into the shawl, together with my pistols and stuffed it all into a saddlebag. The innkeeper had a look of disbelief as I got a foot into the stirrup and swung my leg over to ride astride the saddle. We turned the horses to the road for Kettering and with a wave to the innkeeper and his serving girl we trotted away.

"Tell me, Somerset, how came your friend Kat to Brandeston in 1645?" Gabriel asked. I told him the whole story of the Halloween party and about Jac, even about the police hunt for the missing teenagers. I had to explain quite a lot about my time to him but there was much he already knew from when we were together before. I said what Shelley had told me about the Time Slip and the parallel astral plane.

He seemed to understand all this, telling me about his journey to Naseby and how it was different from the first time. It all pointed to the Lords Temporal making adjustments in time itself so we could join forces and ride for Brandeston. First though, Gubbins said, we would need to do as we had before, the same as I did with Kat. I needed some boy's clothes. It made sense, to ride to Kettering and get me some breeches, a shirt and a coat. That way we could ride faster and be less conspicuous. This time I would be a Puritan boy. We found everything we needed in the market. A good pair of Puritan boots to go with the austere outfit and the puritan hat. No one really paid much attention to our purchase. I suppose they assumed we were shopping for family.

We rode out of Kettering and once on the open road found a big oak tree and some bushes, good cover where I quickly changed into the boy's outfit. It was like old times. Me and Gabriel Gubbins together again. Two boys riding, this time for Brandeston, like blood brothers. Or was it? I wondered at the funny feeling I had when he touched my hand in the market. Then there was the way I felt when he talked about Madeleine. I quickly put this out of my mind. Another thing I had noticed was I was having no problem with my ADHD, my Attention Deficit Hyperactive Disorder. I was with Gubbins and it felt really good.

Our route to Cambridge was much quicker than when I rode to Naseby with Kat and Tom Cobbold. We were coming into Puritan country and no one challenged us. The King had lost the battle and news travels fast, the word of his defeat by Cromwell's New Model Army already spreading wide. We had no idea whether the Witchfinder General had taken Kat and Tom Cobbold to Brandeston but it was a good guess he would. I knew we had left there with Anne Leech and Anne Wright held as witches. I felt sure as well they had hidden Kat's Grimoire somewhere in Brandeston.

We decided the best thing to do was to first head for The Green Man at Grantchester Meadows to see if there was news of Tom Cobbold. If Madeleine was there I was sure she would know what had happened to Tom and Kat. Besides, it would be late and we could break the journey. As we were now Puritans, at least in look, I felt we would be safe near Cambridge, it being Cromwell's area. The Roundheads had won the battle and it was almost certain there would be celebrations, even if it was in Puritan style. We rode steadily, saving the horses and I felt a deep sense of relief we were together and on our way to find and rescue Kat.

17
TORTURE OF THE WITCHES

John Lowes, the Vicar of Brandeston would not break under torture. Not at first. Matthew Hopkins, the Witchfinder General, had returned to Brandeston with his captives, the witch known as Kat and her accomplice, as he stood accused, Tom Cobbold. In his absence Hopkins' assistant, John Stearne, had extracted confessions from the two now named as witches. Anne Leech, known as Mother Leech, and Anne Wright. They confessed their practice of witchcraft and magik. The torture they endured brought them to tell of their friendship with the vicar, John Lowes, and his links to witchcraft. What they did not confess to was knowledge of the whereabouts of Kat's Grimoire.

By the time of his return, Matthew Hopkins was becoming obsessed by the desire to have this book at all costs, so convinced was he that its secrets would bring him great power. He turned his attentions to John Lowes, taking the vicar to Framlingham, where he had his toes tied to his thumbs. The eighty year-old man was thrown into Framingham Mere to see if he would float. He did not. So he was brought to the surface, spluttering and nearly drowned. Whereupon Hopkins, Stearne and Jac made him run continuously back and forth until he was totally exhausted. He was denied sleep for night after night. He was accused of sending an Imp to cause a storm which blew up and sank a ship off the Harwich coast. Many lives had been lost.

Exhausted and wanting only to die, John Lowes confessed to witchcraft. But he never did reveal the whereabouts of the book, Kat's Grimoire. Hopkins, denied this knowledge, had the vicar committed to trial as a witch at Bury St. Edmunds. Angry and frustrated, the Witchfinder General turned his focus back to Mother Leech and Anne Wright; and to Kat and Tom Cobbold.

***

It was late in the evening as we rode across Grantchester Meadows, a picture of peace and tranquillity after our time on the road. Word had already reached The Green Man and the whole of Cambridge of the great Battle of Naseby, the defeat of the King by Oliver Cromwell's New Model Army. Great cheers went up amongst the scholars of the university. Many of them were dining at The Green Man. We tied our horses in the courtyard. I had taken the precaution of keeping my pistols in my belt but they had not been needed. The general atmosphere was that war was over, the King a spent force, his infantry taken prisoner. The Royalist army was no more. Cambridge, a Roundhead town and formerly the seat of Cromwell himself, celebrated in as much Puritan style as was allowed.

We walked into the inn. Madeleine was at the bar, serving tankards of ale. She looked surprised at first, and then seemed genuinely pleased to see us both. I caught Gabriel's gaze upon her and I was not happy with the way he looked at her. Never mind. As she poured us ale he whispered:

"It is she, the one who gave me the trout at Naseby."

"I thought it was so." I said, "She is Tom Cobbold's sister. I think she might be a Traveller, to reach you so quickly and return to Cambridge as she did."

"Perhaps you are right, Somerset, I thought this too, but she has some strange aura I do not understand."

Madeleine asked if we had eaten. She said there was not much but she had some potage left and we were grateful for that. Gabriel paid for two rooms for the night. Madeleine told us she had it on good authority that Kat and Tom Cobbold were indeed being held at the witches' cottage in Brandeston, awaiting an order from the Justices to commit them to trial. Not really knowing how long such things take I prayed we would not be too late. I wanted to go to them but I was really tired and Gubbins said we needed a plan to rescue them. It had been a long day. I told him I wanted to sleep and did he mind if I went to my room? Of course not, he said.

The inn was emptying and I wearily climbed the stairs, happy I had found Gubbins but concerned about Kat. I found, once I got to the room, I could not sleep. So much had happened I should have been able to just put my head on the bolster thing on the bed and go to sleep. But I could not. My mind was racing. I went and sat in the window seat, overlooking the courtyard.

It was still quite warm and the window was ajar. Someone had taken our horses and put them in the stable but there was one horse still tied up. It was then I saw and heard Madeleine walk into the yard with a man. I could not see who it was, in the shadows, but I heard Madeleine say something about Brandeston. The man nodded, got quickly onto the horse, turned and rode fast out of the yard, hooves clattering at first. Then the horse seemed to glide silently over the cobble stones and the image of the horse and rider appeared to become like mist and vanish.

I tried not to think too hard about this but it troubled me. Perhaps the man was just a friend, a boyfriend maybe, saying goodnight. How did he and the horse just disappear? It must have been a trick of the fading light. The thoughts faded as I lay on the bed and fell into a deep sleep.

The following morning I woke up to a familiar sound. A lark was singing. This time I did not hear the dog fox barking. I had fallen asleep still dressed, although I had taken off the Puritan hat. I bundled my hair up and put on the hat and I walked across the landing to the latrine before going downstairs to find Gabriel and something to breakfast.

My pistols were in my belt but a lot of people did the same so no one took any notice. Gabriel had already started and had a platter of food before him. I had forgotten how fit he looked. He seemed older, more mature than the last time I had travelled. Maybe it was the time adjustments that did it. The inn was quite full and talk was about the Battle of Naseby. Who did this and that. Who was shot and injured. Who was dead. How the day was won.

"Word has travelled, with all the talk." I said.

"Aye, perhaps there are others around here who are Travellers and can move in time." Gubbins observed.

"Or witches. They can time travel too." I added. I was beginning to wonder if Madeleine was really one and not a Traveller as she had claimed. Gubbins said she had this strange aura. Where was she from? Her accent was unusual. Was she from Europe somewhere, with her gypsy looks? Tom Cobbold was a pirate, that we knew. Madeleine came to our table.

"Can I fetch you anything? Baken, eggs? There is no trout today."

"Thank you but I am already full and we must get on the road to Brandeston. How far is it?" I asked.

"A days ride at least. We can travel straight. The word is there are no patrols, the King being defeated. Royalist Cavaliers are in hiding. Cromwell rules the country, with the New Model Army and Parliament's support." I thought Madeleine said 'we' can travel. Did that mean she was coming too? I asked her this.

"If my brother is taken to Brandeston then I must find him. The witchfinders seem not to care. They are happy to take the money, witch or not." I felt for her, the same way I was feeling for poor Kat, alone and at the mercy of Matthew Hopkins.

"Then we shall ride together for Brandeston and take what action we can to halt this witchfinder." Gubbins said firmly. "Let us saddle the horses. Madeleine, how will you ride?" He asked.

"I shall wear my brother's clothes and ride like a man, the same as Somerset here." She replied. I really did not like the way they were looking at each other. Jealous? Why should I be jealous? It was not like that with Gubbins. We were friends. Travellers. Fighters for justice and right. There was nothing between us. I thought.

Madeleine cleared the platters and remains of the food while Gubbins and I went to ready the horses. Madeleine joined us, dressed like Tom Cobbold, though not so very pirate-like. Saddled up, we had a good, early start. With food packed in the saddle bags we had no need to stop along the way and we prepared ourselves for the long, hard day's ride ahead.

***

Although there was a witches' Ducking Pond at Framlingham, Matthew Hopkins had chosen Framlingham Mere to 'swim' John Lowes. It was away from the centre of the village, near the road to Wickham Market. Here, out of sight of the authorities, the Witchfinder General subjected the vicar to cruel torture, ducking him time and time again, without too many to see because torture was not legal. Watching in horror though were Kat and Tom Cobbold. Both were recovered from the ordeal at Naseby but living in fear of what was to become of them. Kat saw the poor, spluttering vicar pulled from the water. Jac was standing laughing.

Two witches at Framlingham had linked the vicar to witchcraft. His parishioners had accused him of Papist leanings and being vexatious. On one occasion, it was said, the vicar had hit a parishioner full on the nose, making them bleed profusely. It was not hard for Hopkins and his men to gain the authority in Framlingham to extract a confession from the vicar, who in the end capitulated. Kat and Tom braced themselves for the moment they too would be accused.

But Hopkins did not 'swim' them. He decided to return to Brandeston as his base. There he would see how John Stearne had progressed with the two witches, Anne Leech and Anne Wright. He was also sure that the other witch he sought, the one he knew of as Klaudia together with her friend Gabriel Gubbins would attempt to find her friend Kat. Where else would they look?

The girl Jac, who was proving herself a worthy witch hunter and pricker, confirmed for him this was the most likely. As she put it, Klaudia and Kat were best friends and bound by witchcraft. The sooner they were together the sooner they could be accused and taken to trial. Hanging was the best thing, she said, to end any chance of them wielding a spell, or finding and using the book for their own magik. Jac convinced the Witchfinder she could extract confessions from them and find the book, Kat's Grimoire, for him. She was sure the book was still in Brandeston. He would soon have its power in his hands. So it was they planned to return to the village, to complete the torture of its vicar, swim Kat and Tom, and apprehend Klaudia and Gubbins.

***

We had arrived at Brandeston only to find the Witchfinder General had gone to Framlingham, taking Kat, Tom Cobbold and John Lowes with him. We had quietly tied our horses at the back of the Crossed Swords. Madeleine had left a family friend in charge of the inn and he told us some startling news. All but one or two of Hopkins' soldiers remained at the two Anne's cottage.

Both women had been tortured to near death and confessed to witchcraft but, mysteriously, both had disappeared, vanished before the eyes of witnesses from the village. The villagers, seeing this were in fear of their lives and fled the cottage to their own homes. Even John Stearne became deeply concerned that some inexplicable and evil power now hung over the cottage.

He gathered his men and left for Framlingham, to find Matthew Hopkins and relate what had occurred.

It was very late in the day and there really was no chance of riding on to Framlingham, although it was not that far away. Our horses were very tired so it was better to spare them and set out the following day, when we would be rested as well. Madeleine offered to prepare food but she, Gubbins and I had eaten on the road and we decided it was best to get some sleep. At least I did. I did not realise Gabriel stayed awake and watched over me. There was only one room available in the inn so we had to share. I had barely put my head on the on the long, sausage-like bolster pillow when I was asleep. Gubbins sat on a chair by the window, keeping watch and, although he drifted in and out of sleep, determined to warn me if trouble came.

The night passed without incident. The following morning I decided to dress in women's clothes, the ones I had in my saddlebag. I tucked my pistols into the skirt and wrapped the shawl around me. I noticed as well I still had the little flask of potion the Annes had given me. I tucked it into a pocket. We went downstairs together.

There were one or two looks from local people who came into the inn, but mostly those at breakfast were passing through, Madeleine told us. If anyone was looking out for me they would be looking for a boy. Or so I thought. Still, we should keep alert, even if the Witchfinder was no longer in the village. I noticed the crossed swords were back on the wall above the fireplace, as we walked through to the dining area.

I picked up a plate and covered it with cheese and meat and poured a glass of wine. Why not? Everyone else was drinking wine or ale. We had decided to ride for Framlingham to see if we could find news of the whereabouts of the Witchfinder General. Gubbins, I had noticed, always ate his food much faster than me. He said he would go and get the horses ready. As he crossed the room I realised how much taller he was than I remembered. He was big, powerful-looking in the sense of body build. Very fit. It was like seeing Nathaniel, his brother, except Gubbins was fair haired whilst Nathaniel was dark.

I was really enjoying my breakfast when it happened. Jac was the first to walk into the room.

"Hello Klaudia," she said, as if she was greeting me at school, "long time no see." She acted like some drama student, a bandoleer slung around her shoulder and in her hand a menacing flintlock pistol. I already had a hand on mine but other men had entered the room. Matthew Hopkins, Witchfinder General, John Stearne, witch hunter and four Roundhead soldiers, each with a French Carabine rifle and a pistol. I caught sight of Madeleine. She wore a guilty look. I thought back to the courtyard at The Green Man and the rider. Had she sent him ahead to reach Hopkins? Had she betrayed us? She had a motive. Her brother in exchange for me, and Gubbins. I prayed he would not come back into this ambush.

I was marched out of the inn but not searched. Paraded through the village, people came out of their houses and shouted 'witch, witch, see Mother Leech. She is a witch and she will pay with her neck. For all the wrongs. For the babies dying. For the poor crop. See she disappears and appears at will. Satan is her beloved. The curse of the village goes with her to her death. She brought the disease, the plague to Brandeston. Her and Anne Wright.' One woman held up her baby, a screaming brat whose face was almost purple.

"See what you have done. Cursed my baby. You will rot in hell."

I could not believe they were seeing me as Mother Leech. Surely they must see I was not she. But the thought began to come to me and the gorge rose in my throat. No villagers had seen me before. Now, without my hat and dressed as I was, I remembered I looked quite like Anne Leech, with my dark hair. Then I had a horrible thought. Kat looked very like Anne Wright. Here I was but where was Kat?

It was not long before I found out. We came to the two Anne's cottage and I was pushed roughly through the door. There was Kat, sobbing, and the vicar, sitting in a chair, looking near to death. Some chains were at his feet but he was not tied or manacled. There was no sign of Tom Cobbold. Jac followed me into the cottage with the Witchfinder General and John Stearne. None of the other men would go in. It seemed John Stearne had met up with Hopkins on the road to Framlingham, having lost Mother Leech and Anne Wright in his charge. I could see Matthew Hopkins was not happy with John Stearne but he said:

"We have lost part of our prize. But we will not go empty handed to the Justices in Bury St. Edmunds. These two will pass as Mother Leech and Anne Wright. They may be hanged by the neck for all to see but first they will tell us the whereabouts of the book. Perhaps some leniency may be granted if they do."

Kat looked nervously at me. We both knew he was lying. Once he had the book he could do anything he wanted with us.

"You cannot do this. We are not the two Annes. We are not witches." I shouted at Hopkins and Stearne. Jac started to laugh.

"Of course you are. Why else would you be here. Appearing as you did, out of nowhere. With a book of witches' secrets." She cackled. John Stearne turned to Hopkins.

"Still, it is true, these two are not Mother Leech and Anne Wright, though they look uncommon like them."

Hopkins stared thoughtfully back at the other man.

"They have re-manifested themselves. Changed their bodies to suit their evil purposes of witchcraft and magik. We have swum them, pricked them and they have confessed. Now we will take them to trial. It is within my power and jurisdiction. Tell us the whereabouts of the book." The Witchfinder General wore a cruel smile beneath his moustache and long beard. I realised of course we were trapped. We did not know where Kat's Grimoire had been hidden when the two Annes took it. I made this point.

"Look, we know not of where the book may be. If we knew you could have it." I gave Kat a look, as if to say I was bluffing.

"The two Annes took the book and hid it. You should have found out from them." This was all happening too fast and I was wondering where Gubbins was and what had happened to Tom Cobbold. How had he got away? I soon had the answer. Even though Hopkins had Kat and me he was angry with John Stearne for letting the two Annes out of his charge. Stearne protested and said they had practised magik, that the cottage was enchanted and the Devil himself had made it possible for them to disappear. Then he said to Hopkins:

"What of the pirate? He was in your charge and you let him go."

Hopkins paused for a moment, stroking his beard.

"He too is in league with the Devil. He vanished on the road from Framlingham," he said, a little sheepishly, "there is also no sign of this Gabriel Gubbins. The pirate's sister says he and the witch (he pointed at me) arrived last night together but there is no sign of him."

The bitch, Madeleine, I thought. Couldn't she keep her mouth shut? What did she know of Tom Cobbold's disappearance? Was she a Traveller or was she really a witch? 'Come to me Gubbins.' I shouted in my head. Help us here. And what of Madeleine? Before, they had tried to take her as a witch. Now, it seemed, she was happily in league with Hopkins. Even though her brother had disappeared like a spirit. There was a noise outside the cottage, shouting and then a clash of swords. Gubbins, I hoped. John Stearne went to investigate. I was standing quite close to the vicar. Jac was watching me and had a stupid grin on her face.

"I told you two I would get you," she said, "now you'll die here, along with the other three hundred witches the witchfinders capture and have condemned."

How did she know there were three hundred? I had the passing question in my head. Matthew Hopkins walked to the window to see what was happening. I seized the moment. I shot a look to Kat, cast my eyes down to the chains at the vicar's feet, and back to her. She nodded. We both reached simultaneously for the ends of the chain, picked it up and ran at Jac. We caught her totally by surprise with the chain at her neck and so easily knocked her right off her feet.

Matthew Hopkins came for us and we turned on him, dragging the chain across his shins. He went down. I pulled his sword from his scabbard, lifted his flintlock pistol from his belt and cocked it. I didn't mean it to but it went off. He slumped forwards in a heap. We pulled John Lowes off the chair. He groaned as we pushed him out of the cottage, leaned him against the wall and joined Gabriel Gubbins and Tom Cobbold in fencing Hopkins' men.

Kat had picked up a sword from one of the men who had fallen wounded. There were four of them and we were evenly matched, in numbers and almost in skill. But Gubbins dispatched the man before him with a slicing blow to the side of the neck. Tom Cobbold dropped his man with a cut and thrust across one thigh. He limped back towards the cottage. Kat had her man pinned against the wall, his sword fallen to the ground. She had his own pistol in her hand, aimed at his heart.

I parried the last thrust from John Stearne in front of me, catching his sword and lifting it clean out of his hand. It flew through the air and I caught it in my left hand, sliced the two swords across his front and opened a gash across his chest. The blood began to spill, reddening his white shirt. He too backed off and, pulling the other men, they moved as quickly as they could inside the cottage, slamming the door behind them.

We knew there were many more of Hopkins' men in the village so we quickly got hold of the vicar and steered him in the direction of the church. As we reached it we could hear lots of shouts in the distance, coming from the cottage. It would not be long before

Hopkins' men were in pursuit. We bundled John Lowes into the chancel.

"Where is it? You know where it is," Kat shouted at the vicar, "I can feel it is here, my book. The two Annes gave it to you. Where did you put it?"

"In the tabernacle," groaned the vicar who clearly was past caring about anything. Kat ran to the tabernacle.

"Where's the key?"

"Under the altar cloth, there is a cupboard. In the top a wooden drawer face. Tap it once." The vicar mumbled. She did this and the drawer opened, revealing the key. She quickly opened the tabernacle and reached in. She felt nothing. Frantically she reached deeper but the tabernacle was empty. The book was gone.

18
BEWITCHED

Matthew Hopkins always carried a bible close to his heart. It probably saved his life as the bullet from the flintlock pistol, fired by the witch, Klaudia, had buried itself in the book. It was not luck, it was the will of God himself. The Lord had intervened, saved Hopkins so he might continue his good works. Hunting witches. At least this was his belief and what he told John Stearne as the other man helped the Witchfinder General to his feet. They had lost all their prizes, with the exception of Mary of Yoxford.

The two Annes, in the charge of John Stearne, had mysteriously disappeared from the cottage. The girl-witch, Kat, who was in the likeness of Anne Wright escaped together with the one known as Klaudia, rescued it seemed by the very men they sought. Gabriel Gubbins, and the inn-keeping pirate, Tom Cobbold. He who had witches' power to disappear as well. Hopkins would not rest until he had them all, ready to be tried, found guilty and hanged by the neck until dead.

He stood with his men outside the cottage they all now believed to be bewitched. Secret powers must lie within. Hopkins was right. Brandeston was a village so full of witches it must be a seat of the Devil. Where did these children they were fighting gain the power to defeat them, in sword play as well as in their mystical transformations? No one was in any doubt witchcraft was at the root of it but until now the ones they had seized and accused of being witches were old women and men, none of whom ever fought back. Hopkins swore an oath on his crumpled bible, before his small army of troops, that he would bring these witches to justice. Parliament and England could only thank him for ridding them of these meddling, evil connections with the spirit world. He called upon the men to find the missing witches and bring them to him. The rewards would be bountiful, he promised, and they knew him to be a man of his word. Their numbers had swollen as news had travelled.

Brandeston was a village under the power of witches and leading them was their very own vicar, John Lowes. It was not long before they heard he, the young witches and the two young men had been seen going towards the church. More of Hopkins' men had gathered at the cottage and he despatched the best swordsmen among them. They mounted up and sped through the village.

"The book is not here, you lied. Where is it?" Kat shouted at the vicar.

"As God is my witness, I placed the book in the tabernacle for safekeeping." The old man moaned. Kat began searching the drawer in the altar. There was the sound of horses coming towards the church.

"The secret passage." Tom Cobbold pointed. "Hopkins' men are coming, we must go."

"But the book, we can't go without it. Hopkins must have it. We'll fight them and get it back" My anger was rising to boiling point. A fit was coming.

"Not this day, Somerset. Do as Tom says. If Hopkins has the book we will get it back but now we go." Gubbins pushed me firmly. Without further argument we ran for the hidden door, dragging the vicar between us. We ran along the passage until we came breathlessly to the steps up into the inn. It was then I looked back and realised Gabriel and Tom Cobbold had not followed us down the passage. They must have stayed to fight Hopkins' men.

The trapdoor above us opened and there stood Madeleine. Now my anger really boiled. She had betrayed us, I was sure. It was our turn. The vicar stumbled groggily up the steps ahead of us and flopped into a nearby chair. I waved my sword at Madeleine, who was unarmed.

"Kat, this one is a bitch and has a lot to answer for. Guard her and careful, she is a Traveller or a witch. She can, it seems, disappear at will." I pushed Kat in front of Madeleine. Kat held her sword trained on Madeleine's neck. I walked to a window overlooking the street. There was no sign of Hopkins' men or of Gubbins and Tom Cobbold. I prayed Gubbins was alright.

Tom and his sister were becoming a mystery to me. He disappearing and re-appearing as well as her. Whose side were they really on? It really did seem as if she had betrayed us that morning and yet they both said they wanted revenge on Matthew Hopkins for what he did to their mother. Now Tom had teamed up with Gabriel to defend us. I just wasn't sure anymore what to think. I turned back to Madeleine.

"The truth. What are you? Traveller or witch and why did you not warn me this morning. Who was that fellow in the courtyard at The Green Man? Did you send him to tell Hopkins we were coming?"

Madeleine stood silently looking at me, Kat's sword at her throat. After a long pause she replied.

"I did not betray you but I did not tell you the whole truth. I am Traveller, but not in your sense. I am a witch and so is Tom. The man I sent from Cambridge is a witch also. I sent him to bring news of where Tom and Kat had been taken after Naseby. He came back that night with news they were in Framlingham. Accept my word, I knew not the Witchfinder had returned this morning. It was too late to warn you when he and the one called Jac arrived at the inn. At least Gubbins was not taken as well. I managed to slip word to him so he escaped them."

Kat looked at me and I gave her a nod. She lowered her sword.

"If all that is true, what next?" Kat asked.

"If you are a witch can you help us with a spell to get us both home if we can't Travel? There is some powerful force that has been keeping Kat here." I added.

"It is not as simple as a spell." Said Madeleine. "It is the book you seek that is keeping you here. The book is special, indeed it is the reason you came. I know you have travelled from the future. We are here to help you. Me, Tom, the Annes. The book brought you here, or should I say there were forces at work to bring the book to the Witchfinder General."

"How do you know that?" I looked at Madeleine intently. There was nothing in her face to tell me she was not being truthful. She sighed and motioned us to a table. As we sat down it was as if she was unloading a great weight.

"Your Lords Temporal called to us. Time travellers and witches often move on the same astral plane. This much I know."

"It is how witches can help in the fight against the Time Masters and their plan to rule over Time itself. To change history at will and, more menacingly, to change the future." It was Gubbins' voice from behind me. I swung round and he was there with Tom Cobbold. Gabriel was looking even more handsome I thought.

"And they send Time Violators to create the change."

"'tis true. We are about to witness great change in English history, with the King defeated but still at arms with Cromwell. Matthew Hopkins, the Witchfinder General, has his part to play in this. With the country at war he has had almost free reign to hunt and bring to trial anyone he deems to be a witch." Gubbins replied.

"Are you telling us he has something to do with time travelling? Are you saying he is a Time Violator?" My mind was racing at this thought.

"That may be so," Tom Cobbold cut in. We have seen him rise as if from nowhere. No one really knows where he came from. Yes it is said he is from Manningtree, the son of a vicar, but the evidence of his early life is flimsy, almost non-existent."

"And we know why he wants the Grimoire." Everyone turned to Gubbins.

"Hopkins has moved through the counties with almost military precision, finding and accusing common folk with witchcraft. He has virtually his own army of followers, soldiers, prickers and henchmen to perform the 'swimming' tests. But he knows he is hardly catching any real witches to torture, most have been too clever to be taken by him. He and a Time Master, together with Jac, drew you both here with the book. So he can take advantage of its secrets."

"What is it that's so special?" I asked Gabriel but it was Madeleine who gave the answer.

"The book is believed to hold secret all the names of all the real witches, oracles, soothsayers and Travellers of all time, past present and future. It could give the Witchfinder and his masters the key to complete power to hunt down and to manipulate time travel for their own evil ends.

"And if they possess the many secrets of the book it may unleash devastation in the world. The Civil War will become a paltry skirmish in comparison." Tom Cobbold added.

There was complete silence around the table. Suddenly it was clear. Kat's book could be the most dangerous force in the world, even in the universe.

"Then we must destroy the book, when we find it." I said.

"To do that, even if it could be done, would bring greater destruction to the world. The book is almost a living thing, a collection of souls." Gabriel looked more serious than I had ever seen him.

"How do you know all this, Gabriel? I asked.

"The Voices have told me. Every living person is a traveller. We are born, learn, live, spend time on this earth. We are all passing through, like travellers to this inn. Tomorrow we could be gone. We know not what destiny may hold for us but we are free in our destiny, for as long as we are here. To make choices, to think and follow our instincts.

"Cromwell wants England to be free of the constraints of the rule of King Charles 1. He has nothing against the King himself, only what he stands for. It is the same. We cannot allow the Time Masters to rule and change Time, purely for their own gain, because they believe they have some divine right to do so. The Voices tell me it is why we are here, each of us, to fight evil. The Grimoire must survive, as must we, to return the book to its rightful guardians at that point in future time. Kat's mother and Kat herself. For she is the next witch in line to learn the mysteries it holds." Gubbins eloquent speech left us with our mouths open, lost for words.

We placed our hands on the table, one on top of another and swore allegiance to the Lords Temporal, witches, Travellers and Time itself. We five.

19
WOBURN ABBEY

"You must go, ride for London and Parliament. Carry the news of what the Witchfinder General has perpetrated on the people hereabouts. Petition to have him stopped and the laws changed." Tom Cobbold hustled us towards the horses, already saddled and loaded with provisions for our journey. Gabriel had agreed we would ride for London but en route we would find a friend of his father's, to help us draw up a petition. Someone with legal background and knowledge of how to approach Parliament. He did not say who this friend was, only that he thought it would be important and lend weight to our cause.

We mounted up and bade our goodbyes to the vicar, Tom and Madeleine. They said they would take the vicar to some safe haven, away from Brandeston and the witchfinders. We turned the horses onto the road out of Brandeston, Kat and I dressed again as boys, French Carabines in our scabbards, pistols at the ready. We both still had the witches' potion. Kat had kept her flask as well. Although we had not used any, and didn't know exactly what it could do, it gave us some reassurance it might ward off spiritual dangers we might encounter.

As we left the village we heard, in the distance, the sound of many horses' hooves clattering through the streets. I looked back and could see people coming out of their houses. I was sure the witchfinders must be looking for us and would find the vicar, Tom and

Madeleine at the inn.

"We must go back and help them." I said to Gubbins.

"There is little we can do, we are outnumbered and would only be taken ourselves. Perhaps they have hidden in the secret passage. The Witchfinder and his men know not of that for we led them away from the church before we came to the inn to find you. Tom and I paid some young men to ride out of the village, as if it were us, and the Roundheads went in pursuit."

"But there must be something we can do." Kat uttered as we broke into a gallop.

"Better we get as far from here as we can and ride as we planned. We will return from London and Parliament with authority to stop the practice of witchhunting. If they are caught and held, we will petition the Justices for their release."

Gabriel led the way like some charging Cavalier and our horses dutifully raced with his through the countryside. Eventually we slowed the horses to a walk, now we were well away from Brandeston, indeed from Suffolk. In all that had happened I had not thought until then how Gabriel and Tom Cobbold came to be together to rescue us.

"When the girl Jac and the soldiers took you at breakfast," he told us, "I was saddling the horses in the courtyard when Tom appeared. Madeleine came running to tell me you had been taken. They told me they were witches both and wanted only to help us stop the witch hunts. Tom, on the road from Framlingham, had a witch's potion, given to him by Mother Leech. He deceived the Witchfinder General and his men by using it to stop time for a moment. They did not witness him ride away but he could not take Kat with him."

"One second he was riding alongside me then he was gone." Kat confirmed.

"Madeleine told us you had been taken to the Annes' cottage so we came after you." Gubbins pulled up his horse. We had reached a crossroads with a stone signpost for London but we did not turn onto the London road. We were heading for Bedford, the way Kat and I had ridden with Tom Cobbold when we were escaping from Captain Dagger and his troops.

"It is where my father's friend is." Was all Gubbins would impart.

"Do you think Parliament will listen to us?" Kat asked him.

"With recommendation from the right people they should hear what we have to say. I know from my brother Nathaniel, who is an Intelligencer for the Cause, there is concern amongst many over the practices of the Witchfinder General. He is not, as he claims, officially appointed to carry out his witch hunts. He preys on the superstitions of a people at war. Blame must be found for all that is ill and to point the finger at supposed witches is easy for common folk. That intelligent people in high office in the towns of East Anglia are relieved of large sums of money by Hopkins beggars belief. But these are strange times. There are some though, in Parliament, already petitioning against Hopkins. We will find them and join voices."

"We don't have long." I said. Kat and Gabriel stared at me.

"I remember now, Mr. Payne telling us in our history lesson. The Battle of Naseby was in June 1645. Where we are now."

"Don't have long for what?" Kat asked.

"To petition in London and go back to Bury St. Edmunds."

"We can't go back there, we're wanted by the Justices."

"When they learn what happened we will be alright." I felt sure it would be so.

"Somerset, why do we not have long?" Gabriel echoed Kat's question.

"Because the witch trials at Bury St. Edmunds in 1645 will be held in July and sentences passed by August. On the twenty seventh of August 1645 eighteen people will be hanged as witches. One of them will be John Lowes, the Vicar of Brandeston. I remember reading it."

"You're right, I remember now," said Kat, "and some of the others accused by Hopkins as witches were Mary Clowes of Yoxford..."

"With Anne Leech and Anne Wright." The whole lesson came flooding into my head. A special court had been set up for the trial, instigated by the Witchfinder General.

We had turned onto the road towards Woburn. The horses were tired, as were we three. Kat was slumped forward in the saddle, almost asleep.

"This friend of your father's, Gabriel, who is he?" Gubbins told us at last, saying it was better we had not known before we arrived at Woburn, in case we were challenged on the journey.

"The man is in favour with neither the Roundheads nor the Cavaliers. He is Lord William Russell, Earl of Bedford." Gabriel said.

"He may not be too pleased to see us."

"Why is that, Somerset?"

"On the way to Naseby we were caught sleeping in one of his barns, by his gamekeeper. He could recognise us."

"Why would that be a worry?" Gabriel smiled at me.

"Because we threatened to shoot him." Said Kat who had woken up.

"Ah, trouble walks with you. Worry not. I will be the spokesperson. The Earl owes my family a favour. I will apologize on your behalf and all will be well." Gubbins led the way as we rode a long, majestic drive. Well, it was more of a track really. The abbey rose into view as we approached. The house was not like the one in my time, it was still church-like. I did not notice at first. Riders had appeared behind us and then I saw ahead, the same gamekeeper, Thomas Jones, with a musket aimed squarely at us.

"I know you two. You Sir, you too seem familiar. What is your business here?"

"I am Gabriel Gubbins, son of Sir Marmaduke Gubbins, come to see Lord Russell with news of the King's defeat at The Battle of Naseby. You will inform His Lordship we are here and put down the musket, it is not even cocked."

Jones obediently did what Gabriel told him and walked off into the house. Kat looked at me and we nodded in agreement. He did look fit.

Suddenly there were servants emerging from the building and as we dismounted our horses were led away by a groom for a well-earned rest. We were shown into a big room which was very like a chapel, with stained glass windows. There were tapestries hanging on the walls, depicting battles with foot soldiers, cavalry and canons. You could see the house had been a proper abbey but it had been made into a home and was welcoming, if not warm.

I was surprised when Lord Russell walked into the room. I had imagined he would be an old man but he was a young, dashing, Cavalier type, dressed in a red and gold doublet with matching breeches and grey boots. He had a white lace kerchief around his neck and shoulders. His hair was long, dark and quite curly. I'm not very good at ages but I thought he was not yet thirty years old. I made a mental note to look him up on Wiki when I got home. We sat on big, comfortable chairs. Tea was brought to us and it was all very civilised.

"News travels fast. We heard of the King's defeat at Naseby," the Earl began, "and what of your father? I owe him a favour or two."

"He fought on the side of Parliament and is well rewarded for his efforts. Unlike when he was with the King's troop." Gubbins had introduced us as boys, me being his cousin, Somerset and Kat as a friend from Oxford, named James. But the Earl bellowed a laugh at this and said his gamekeeper had already told him we were girls and that he had found us sleeping in one of the Earl's barns. The Earl seemed very amused by this.

"Both pretty young women I hear, when not dressed as boys." He said.

Gubbins told Lord Russell about the Witchfinder General and what was happening in Suffolk. He was concerned but he pointed out he had just a year earlier decided to withdraw from politics, the fighting and the War. He agreed he would sign a petition to members of Parliament he knew were championing a cause against witch hunting but he would not, as Gubbins suggested come with us to London.

He told us we should contact the writer John Dillingham and Robert White, the publisher of the Moderate Intelligencer, a Parliamentary paper which was having much influence with the members. John Dillingham, Lord Russell said, was unmatched in his connections with Parliamentary and army leaders, and what he wrote was fair and honest. We must, he said, arrange to meet him and tell him all of what Matthew Hopkins was about. Gubbins had not doubted for a moment the Earl would invite us to stay. We dined in fine style on suckling pig and Spanish wine, our host insisting we should be well fed to fortify us for our journey to London.

"You must stay at Bedford House, my London home," he said, "though I don't use it often there is a cook there and a caretaker." We thanked him for this. He told us about his time with the Parliamentarian army, when he fought at the Battle of Edgehill in 1642, the year before I first Travelled and met Gabriel.

The Earl was a leader in the 'Peace Party', a group of Parliamentarians who sought to make peace with the King, but the move was rejected by the Earl of Essex and Lord Russell decided to take sides with the King. The King's daughter, Princes Henrietta, was born in the Earl's town house in Exeter, also known as Bedford House, in 1644. But he became disillusioned with the King and went back to the Parliamentarians. They did not trust him and refused to allow him to retake his seat in the House of Lords.

So he retired to Woburn. The abbey, he told us, had been built by Cistercian monks in 1157 but was taken by King Henry VIII. In his will, the King instructed his son, Edward, to give the abbey to Sir John Russell.

After the meal all we really wanted to do was sleep and we each had our own room. No sooner than I had said goodnight to Gabriel and Kat I was tumbling into a giant four-poster bed with a silk canopy and drapes and I fell fast asleep.

I was awoken in the morning by servants filling a wooden bath tub with hot water in the bedroom. I had to admit, I was very smelly. Mostly, in 1645, you only washed the parts of you that would be seen: face, neck, hands. It was more important to have clean linen clothes. If you had a lot of clean linen you were seen as high in social status.

Many people believed if you took a bath it would let 'bad air' into the pores. But rich people had baths in their bedroom and I was grateful for this. A servant had lined the bath with linen so I would not get any splinters. As she handed me the soap she said it had come all the way from Castile in Spain and was made from olive oil. Well, it felt good and I was smelling a lot better when Kat knocked on the door.

"Klaudia, you must come and see this, there is a grotto, all made with shells."

I don't know how the monks stood for it but even in June the abbey was cold, even colder as I stepped out of the bath shivering. I quickly dried and dressed and followed Kat downstairs. We walked across to a building newer than the rest of the abbey and there it was. The grotto. We stepped inside and I realised I had been there before but in our own time when I went on a trip to Woburn. It was like a beautiful undersea cavern with dolphins swimming and pictures made with sea shells.

"My father had it built for my mother." The Earl had walked in behind us. I really wanted to say the grotto is still there in my time but of course I could not. We walked back to the abbey's dining hall and Gabriel was there. We were spoiled for choice with the food and really stuffed our faces. Lord Russell had written a petition for us to take to Parliament. He said that because he had changed sides between Royalists and Parliamentarians a few times his word would not count for much in some circles but he had some contacts he trusted and he wrote down the names. The horses were saddled and ready to go. Although it had been quite cold in the abbey, outside was a warm morning and we left Lord Russell and Woburn bathed in a pool of sunshine. I tried to describe to Gubbins how different the abbey looked in my time but that was hard. We arrived in Woburn village and turned onto the road for London.

20
JAC

Jacqueline Hamilton-Smith, Jac, as she was known, had sensed her power growing ever stronger since her arrival in 1645. Descended from an ancient family of Travellers, she answered only to the Time Masters and her Caller, Matthew Hopkins, Witchfinder General. She was essential to their plan to seize Kat's Grimoire and unlock its secrets. When Jac time-travelled to 1645, bringing Kat with her, she knew it would lure Klaudia Cay into coming after her and she knew as well Klaudia would bring the book with her. Such was the power of the Time Masters and Jac was drawing on that power.

Jac first realised she could move around in immediate time and space when she disappeared from the witches' cottage to join the Witchfinder's company of followers. Now she was not simply a Traveller, she could appear and disappear at will. Something she knew Klaudia had not yet developed the power to do. But Jac did know Klaudia's other powers were equal, if not greater than her own. She had witnessed Klaudia, in another time send a Time Violator to Oblivion. But at this moment the Time Masters were in control.

It was they who had sent Gabriel Gubbins to Naseby when the Lords Temporal allowed him to travel to find Klaudia. They were preventing Klaudia from moving around in time and finding a way home. Jac would work with them to make sure Klaudia and Kat would never go home. They would die in 1645, accused and condemned for witchcraft. To seal their fate needed just one thing. Kat's Grimoire. If Jac could find it the Witchfinder would have all he needed. She had proved to him her value as a 'pricker'. Now she would bring him the ultimate prize.

She had learned the importance of the book from Hopkins, who was well aware of the secrets it could reveal. Not only the names of all the *living* witches and sorcerers of England, Scotland and Wales. That was only the start. The Witchfinder would have all he needed when the Time Masters empowered him to travel. To any place and time, past, present or future, to fulfil his destiny as the greatest witch hunter of all time.

The book. Jac knew if she could find it she too would bathe in the glory. The Witchfinder richly rewarded those who helped his quest. The Time Masters had told Jac that Klaudia had arrived at the witches' cottage with the book. But neither the Annes nor the vicar, even under the severe torture inflicted by John Stearne and Jac herself, had revealed its whereabouts. But Jac had a devious plan.

Jac was riding with Hopkins' men as they charged through the village, arriving only moments too late to stop Klaudia, Gubbins and Kat making their escape from Brandeston. Hearing the approaching riders, Tom Cobbold, Madeleine and John Lowes, the vicar, moved as fast as they could. But the old man, having endured the torture of being swum and made to walk back and forth for hour upon hour, was slow on his feet.

With barely seconds to spare they managed to reach the secret passage. Tom and the vicar disappeared down the steps, leaving Madeleine to lower the trapdoor and await the arrival of Hopkins' men. They surrounded the inn, posted like sentries as the Witchfinder marched through the door to confront the young woman before him.

"Where are they? Hopkins demanded.

"Who do you seek?" Madeleine hedged.

"You know well Mistress Cobbold." Hopkins retorted angrily.

"They are all gone. Search for them if you like but they are all gone to London, with a petition to stop you and the witch hunting."

"Take her away, she is a witch." A bloodied John Sterne commanded two stout Roundheads.

"What good will that be? It is better I am here. If I were not, when they return, it would be a warning to them. And return they will. Besides, who will order the ale and serve you. Who will cook good trout and potage to feed your men?"

Hopkins could see the sense of this and he put a hand on Sterne's shoulder.

"Let her be. Leave men to watch her." Hopkins and Sterne, followed by Jack, left the inn, gathering their troop. The Witchfinder, for the first time, had found himself with just one accused witch to take to Bury St. Edmunds. He had no idea when those who had slipped his net would return. Supporting his troop was costing him dear.

"We must find new commissions, more witches to convict to support our cause." He spoke his thoughts openly. Jac smiled to herself, knowing she could provide the means and reap the rewards for helping Matthew Hopkins become the greatest and most feared, witch hunter the world had ever seen.

21
LONDON

London had been abandoned by King Charles 1 after his failed attempts to take back the city from the Parliamentarians. The King had moved his court and headquarters to Oxford in 1643.

Two years later we rode into a London in celebration of the glorious victory at Naseby. Riding through the city Gabriel told us he knew from his brother Nathaniel, who was often there for the 'Cause', the mood of the city had grown cheerful and confident, even though many who had been led by John Pym were trying to impose Puritan restrictions, such as closing the theatres.

Since the King had left, Londoners built massive fortifications with a deep ditch nine feet wide and a rampart all around the city. Forts of rammed earth were erected and cannons were placed everywhere.

Dutch engineers had been brought in to direct the work and everyone from merchants, shopkeepers, silk men, women and girls carried buckets to help the building. Oyster women worked alongside Members of Parliament and lawyers, tailors, watermen, shoe makers and porters, carrying pickaxes, spades and shovels. More than twenty thousand men became part of the Trained Bands, the volunteers of working people who would help defend the city if it was attacked.

As we rode we passed taverns, with people drinking cheerfully outside in the warm evening air. There were women shouting their wares, like we had seen at Bury. Fishwives in Billingsgate, fruit and vegetable sellers in

Covent Garden. We came to Lord Russell's Bedford House and were greeted by Frances, the housekeeper and cook, who made us very welcome, fussing about and offering us tea and food. She showed us our rooms which were light and airy, with four-poster beds and chamber pots. Each room had pretty drapes on the windows, a basin and a fireplace made up but not lit as it was quite warm. We unloaded what little we had from our saddle bags and the horses were led by a young lad to stables in the mews at the back of the house.

Now we were standing in the rather dull entrance hall, which was made so by the wood panelling on the walls. There was a knock at the door and Frances opened it to take a note from a grubby-looking young fellow. She slipped him a coin and handed the paper to Gabriel.

"It is from Nathaniel, my brother, he is in London and bids us join him at the Palsgrave Head, a tavern in the Strand. Come, we will hire a carriage."

I should tell you about Nathaniel Gubbins. The first time I met him was in 1643 and he was the handsomest fellow. One you would not mind being seen with. Nathaniel was an Intelligencer for the 'Cause.' They were people, both Cavaliers and Roundheads, who were working together to try and end the English Civil War. Nathaniel was, as I remember, one day a Cavalier and the next day a Roundhead. I suppose that made him a spy.

The carriage rattled and jolted its way through the London streets. I had to laugh. Our teeth were chattering it was so uncomfortable as it had no springs. The driver seemed to take great pleasure in driving at breakneck speed, the horses' hooves clattering like machine gun fire. Kat was wide eyed, seeing a city, London, in the 1640's for the first time, with all the pretty wooden framed buildings piled on top of each other like higgledy-piggledy little boxes. We passed through narrow little streets of shops, the cobblers, confectioners, silver smiths and candlestick makers.

At last we came into the Strand, relieved our shaky journey was at an end. Gabriel paid the carriage man and we walked into the Palsgrave Head to see, to our surprise, Cavaliers and Parliamentarians drinking together, with bawds and harlots surrounding them for entertainment. This tavern was just as smelly as the ones I had been to in Oxford in 1643.

The hairs on the back of my neck stood up as someone from behind put a hand on my shoulder. My hand went for my sword, but I was spun round firmly to see the laughing face of Nathaniel Gubbins.

"Well, Somerset, we meet again." He took my hand and gave me his usual crushing handshake (remember I was dressed as a boy).

"Nathaniel, it *is* you, how did you know we were in London?" I had been wondering this since Gabriel received the note.

"Lord Russell sent word to the 'Cause' to say you were at his house in London." He turned to Kat.

"And who be this person?"

"James." I said, before Kat could say a word "but really it's Kat, my friend." I whispered to him. He nodded in acknowledgement.

"You came seeking to petition Parliament over this man Matthew Hopkins, the one who calls himself the Witchfinder General." Nathaniel directed to Gabriel.

"We do. Hopkins and his assistant, John Stearne

have brought a reign of terror across Essex, Suffolk and Norfolk, even as far as Northampton."

"The Cause know well of this and questions have been asked in Parliament. We have heard Hopkins uses the 'swimming test' and other torture to gain all his confessions."

"We have seen it ourselves. We saw him torture women, Anne Leech and Anne Wright." I said.

"And I saw him 'swim' an old man, the Vicar of Brandeston." Kat added.

"There are two men here, known to Lord Russell, who must hear your story. The writer John Dillingham and Robert White, the publisher of the Moderate Intelligencer. Both men are influential with Parliament and the army." Nathaniel led us to a booth and the two men rose to greet us. Nathaniel made the introductions before calling over a serving wench and ordering tankards of ale.

We began telling John and Robert about the witchfinders, revealing we were actually girls, not boys as we were dressed. They understood the need for us to travel as boys. They listened intently as we related everything we knew, about the torture, false accusations and the pain inflicted by the witchfinders' 'prickers.'

Suddenly there was a commotion in the tavern which interrupted us. A group of Cavaliers and Roundheads were gathered and cavorting with several women whose faces were heavily made up, their cheeks rouged in contrast to the white of their skin revealed by their low cut, laced bodices but nearly matching the red of their skirts. Punks, Nathaniel called them, the name they used for whores. A Cavalier was arguing with a Roundhead over one of the punks, claiming her for himself. I was staring at the Cavalier and, too late, I realised he had caught my gaze. He broke away from the group, pushing aside the punk and the Roundhead as he strode towards us, looking a little shaky on his feet, probably because of the ale he had been drinking.

"I know you two," he addressed Kat and me, "you are deserters and horse thieves, you were on the road with me, as Royalist Musketeers. Turncoats now as well I see." Captain Dagger came for me. I had my sword in my hand, ready, when a silence came over the tavern. Then the sound of sharp steel as many swords were drawn. Kat was beside me as were Gabriel and Nathaniel, both holding pistols as well as swords. Captain Dagger realised he was facing us alone. He backed off.

"Mark my words, I will have you for desertion and stealing horses." he said.

"Stealing our own horses and desertion from an army that, after Naseby, no longer exists?" I challenged. This raised laughter in the tavern, as people turned back to their drinking. Captain Dagger spun on his heels and walked out, turning back to say, just as he left: "You have not heard the last of me." I sensed, somehow, he might be right.

A short while later we too left. Robert White had told us of a splendid banquet to be held the following day, at Grocer's Hall in Princes Street, in honour of the Parliaments and in celebration of the victory at Naseby. He said all the important Members of Parliament would be there and that we should come to meet one who was particularly interested in the Witchfinder General. We agreed and shook hands on it.

Nathaniel melted away, ghost-like into the crowds

of London's street and Gabriel found us a carriage for another rattling, jolting ride, back to the Bedford house.

***

Jac was ready to execute her plan. She had worked out the timing of her arrival with Kat at the witches' cottage. Now she had to project herself back through time to that moment, and wait. The trick though was to avoid disappearing with her 'real' self from the cottage to join the Witchfinder General, as she had done before Klaudia arrived.

Jac had never tried this before and, she thought for a moment, it may not work. She had to Travel on a different astral plane. It was dangerous because she would be seeing herself with Kat and the witches, but she could not let them see her. If she were to appear, the witches would know what she was doing and a single spell could cause her 'real self' to converge with her astral body.

Were that to happen or worse, should her real self see her astral personification, it could be disastrous. If fusion of the two sides of her were to occur, whichever was the most dominant side could take over. And if that turned out to be the side of her that had returned to the cottage, the worst could happen. She would simply cease to exist.

She would be careful and control her emotions and mood, not allowing any part of her become more dominant over the other.

She had arrived. She could see herself eating potage with Kat and the witches. She saw the moment she Travelled, just disappearing, to join Matthew Hopkins. Her 'other self' remained to witness Klaudia's arrival.

Her adversary was clutching Kat's Grimoire. Jac smiled to herself as she saw the witches lighting sleep-inducing candles to send Klaudia and Kat into dreamland.

The witches removed the book from Kat's grip and Jac followed them as they left the cottage. There was a heart-stopping moment when Anne Leech turned and looked straight at her, a puzzled look on her face, as if she sensed something was there. But she did not see Jac. The witches walked on to the church. Jac watched John Lowes, the vicar, take the key from the secret drawer in the altar and open the tabernacle, placing Kat's Grimoire inside. Now she knew where it was hidden. The problem was, she could not simply take it and return to her present time. She would have to travel forward to her normal self. Then she could seize the prize for the Witchfinder General.

***

The City of London had spared no expense in creating the most splendid banquet for the victorious Parliamentarians. I had never seen so many suckling pigs being roasted in one place. Serving girls in smart uniforms of white laced bodices appeared at the tables with tray after tray of boars' heads with apples in their mouths, cooked capons, turkeys and geese. There were fried oysters, black puddings, mutton pies, rabbit potages and roasted pheasant. Wine was flowing freely.

We had found a corner with Robert White and John Dillingham, who introduced us to another vicar, John Gaule of Great Staughton, and Valentine Walton, a colonel in the Parliamentarian army, Member of Parliament and married to Oliver Cromwell's sister.

Both men were distraught at hearing of the torture of

women and old men at the hands of the Witchfinder General. John Gaule vowed to preach from the pulpit against Matthew Hopkins. Colonel Walton agreed to take our petition all the way to the top, to Oliver Cromwell himself and all the leading members of Parliament he knew were opposed to witch hunting.

The food kept arriving, French dishes, Gabriel pointed out, flavoured with anchovies and capers, partridge cooked in red wine, broiled chine of salmon, lobster, buttered shrimps and spatchcock eels. This all served with raw vegetables and salats, fruit, cheeses and coffee. Kat and I couldn't help stuffing ourselves.

Nathaniel asked how it was so many towns and villages called upon the Witchfinders' services. John Gaule said he had experience in his own parish of the fear of witchcraft.

"They conclude," he said, "there are witches in every place and parish. Every old woman with a wrinkled face, a furrowed brow, a hairy lip, a gobbler tooth. Any with a squint eye, a squeaking voice or a scolding tongue, having a rugged coat on her back, a skull cap upon her head, a spindle in her hand. Any with a dog or cat by her side is not only suspected but pronounced for a witch."

"'tis true, every new disease, accident or judgement of God is accounted for no other but an act or effect of witchcraft." Added Valentine Walton, who also came from Great Staughton. "I have seen much evidence of this in the parish. Parliament will hear our voices on this matter, though be prepared for the wheels of justice to turn slowly. The Members have much to deal with as a consequence of the war. The suppression of witch hunting is not high on their agenda. If Matthew Hopkins is practising within the law there is little to stop him at present.

"An appeal to the Justices of the Assizes may carry weight if it has Parliaments' seal. I can arrange that much and you will have it on the morrow to convey to the courts. It will be on the grounds that you have witnessed the Witchfinder practising torture to extract confessions, which is against the law. Such a document will also secure your innocence in your little, shall we say from what you have told me, 'adventure' in Bury St. Edmunds." Colonel Walton smiled as he looked from Kat to me. "I am told you are uncommon good swordsmen for two women so young. Where learned you the skills?" He had a twinkle in his eyes that told me he'd known all along we were girls dressed as men.

"Gabriel Gubbins taught me." I waved a hand in Gabriel's direction.

"And I learned from Somerset." Said Kat.

"I will have the appeal delivered, where stay you?"

"At the Bedford house." Replied Gabriel. "We will leave for Bury tomorrow."

"Then may God go with you." Said John Gaule.

"Ah, quaking pudding, my favourite." Valentine's eyes lit up like a child's at the sight of the wobbly blancmange with rose water, brought by a serving girl. We raised our glasses of wine.

"To the end of witch hunting." Proposed Valentine.

"To the end of witch hunting." We toasted.

The following day the Parliamentary appeal arrived in the form of a sealed letter, brought to us by Nathaniel, as we were preparing for the journey to Bury

St. Edmunds. What was disturbing was the news he brought as well of the Witchfinder General. Hopkins was claiming he had a book, one he had cheated out of the possession of the Devil himself, with the names of all the witches of England. Kat and I looked at each other, dumbstruck.

"Can it be?" I mouthed. "Gabriel, it must be Kat's Grimoire. We have to get it back. We must go straight to Brandeston."

"We will, Somerset, we will." He assured us as we saddled the horses and said our goodbyes to Frances, the cook.

"I will accompany you to the city wall for safe passage." Nathaniel offered.

"Will you ride with us for Brandeston?" I asked him.

"Nay, I must reside here for there is much to do for the Cause. The King is rallying again, convinced he will re-build his army. I have heard he wrote to Lord Raglan: 'I am nowise disheartened by our late misfortune.' He believes with Irish help he will be in 'far better condition than at any time since the rebellion began.' This, even though he surrendered 4,500 men, all his guns and five hundred horses at Naseby. I hear tell though of four thousand men of Parliament's New Model Army deserted after the battle, so this will give the King confidence."

We had ridden out of the mews towards the city wall when we came upon column after column of bedraggled men, Royalists, walking into the city, escorted by the Trained Bands.

"The King's confidence would be pierced by this sight." Said Nathaniel. "These are Royalists, prisoners from the battle, three thousand of them, I am informed.

I'll wager they will be offered the chance to join Parliament's army in Ireland. Or perhaps they will serve the Spanish King in the Netherlands. If they choose otherwise they will remain prisoners and rot until the war is decided."

We passed stream after stream of soldiers wearing desolate looks and nursing wounds. Most of them were Welsh and far from home. I had to feel sorry for them. They had fought for the King, lost, and he was abandoning them for the Irish.

Our arrival at the limits of the city, the ramparts manned with troops, halted our progress for a while as the entrance was open to allow the prisoners filling the road to limp their way to their uncertain future. Nathaniel bade us farewell and good luck in our quest for the Grimoire and justice in the face of terror wielded by the Witchfinder General. We were on our way to Bury St. Edmunds, fully armed and ready for a fight if any came our way. I smiled at Kat who returned the look.

"We're going to win, Kat, then we'll go home and all this will be just like a dream." I said.

"More like my worst nightmare." She retorted.

"Dream or nightmare, this much is true," Gabriel said as he kicked his horse into a canter, "we three can help save many more innocents being accused of witchcraft. Swear we will bring down this Witchfinder General. Without the book he will be hard pressed to uncover the real witches of England. We ride to save the book."

"The book," we enjoined, each of us raising our hands, high five style.

"How long before we reach Brandeston?" I asked.

"Two day's ride for sure. We will find an inn on the way to stay tonight." Gubbins smiled at me. We had stayed in many inns together when I time travelled before. It put me in mind of why he had 'Called' me.

"What happened in 1647 that made you call me, so soon after we had fought to save the King and Cromwell from assassination, Gabriel?"

He paused for a moment before answering.

"The King thought there was a plot by the Levellers to take his life and he disappeared from Hampton Court, where we had left him under house arrest. I called for your help again but found you were here in 1645."

"How did you know where we were?"

"The Voices told me it was where you would be and that I could Travel to find you, but some power sent me to Naseby again."

"Time Masters." I said, emphatically, "they are controlling the Witchfinder General and Jac, I'm sure of it. Your Voices are the Lords Temporal. Now I can hear them too."

Kat, who had remained silent since we left the London ramparts, suddenly exclaimed:

"The book, it's talking to me. I know where it is."

"With the Witchfinder General, in Brandeston?"

"Yes, but something has happened, someone has opened it, Hopkins has the witches' names."

"Are you sure? How can the book be talking to you?" I asked, sceptically

"The same way you and Gabriel hear the Voices. It must be an astral plane." Kat sounded indignant.

"Then we are going to the right place. Once we have the book we can continue to the Justices of the Assizes at Bury." Gabriel kicked his horse into a canter and we followed, along the old Roman road north. I looked back, briefly, at the city of London on the horizon and I saw riders following in the distance, but we were leaving them behind and I thought no more of it.

***

Jac had wasted no time the day Klaudia, Kat and Gubbins had escaped from the Crossed Swords. She stole a backward glance to make sure she was not being followed. She had arrived at the church at dusk and was standing before the altar. She reached down to lift the altar cloth and pressed firmly on the secret drawer front. It slid open, revealing the tabernacle key which she took and inserted in the lock, turning it easily and opening the door. She reached inside and felt around. Her hand landed on nothing. No book. How could that be? She had seen the vicar place it in the tabernacle. She felt around again but it definitely was not there.

A sudden noise in the eerie silence of the church made her jump. She ducked behind a pillar, concealed from the view of Tom Cobbold and the vicar, John Lowes, emerging through the door to the secret tunnel. The vicar was leading the way, unsteadily, towards the sacristy, the room where the priest and his attendants vest and prepare for the service. Here was kept the chalice, cruets, the altar linens and holy oils. It was also home to the parish register.

Jac slipped through the shadows and overheard John Lowes saying to Tom Cobbold:

"I remember now, I moved the book when I heard there were Puritans in the area removing statues and other icons from the churches, lest the tabernacle was taken as well."

He took a key, one of many, from his belt and unlocked a cupboard standing next to the sacristy credens where the vestments were stored. He reached inside and there, amongst the parish registers, was Kat's Grimoire. He turned and handed it to Tom who immediately felt its power in his hands.

"Come, let's away from here." Tom Cobbold half-whispered as if they might be overheard, which they were as Jac stepped out of the shadows.

"Thank you, I'll take the book now."

"Over my dead body." Uttered Tom

"Then so be it," echoed the voice of the Witchfinder General around the church, as he appeared behind Jac, with John Stearne and the whole troop of Roundheads. Jac marched forward and took the book from the Tom, turned and handed it to Hopkins. He held it in reverence as he gazed at the pentangle on the front cover. Tom Cobbold counted nine men all told. He felt the vicar's hand on his as he reached for his sword.

"Not this day, go, the back door the parish clerk uses is open, go," ushered the vicar under his breath.

Tom Cobbold looked straight at the vicar, as if to say I will come back and find you. Then he was gone, not by the back door but with the speed of a Traveller.

22
THE GRIMOIRE

The priest called upon the Seven Steps: Stones, Fire, Plants, Animals, Man, the Starry Heavens and the Angels. He had surrounded himself with pottery figures of the Deities, Utug, the Dweller of the Desert, who would steal you away if you ventured too far. Telal, the Bull Demon, Alal the Destroyer, Namatar, the god of Pestilence and Inpa, the god of fever.

Witchcraft has existed since time began. Some say the first witch appeared in the time of the Aegyptians and the Pyramids. Others that it was Cham or Zoreaster, but he came much later. This priest had before him tablets of Cuneiform writing, and he was living in the city of Uruk, in Mesopotamia in the year 3100 BC. On some of these tablets were the beginnings of written history. But the priest was not just an historian, though his practise made him eminently suitable for that task.

He was a witch and among the first to write down the incantations of earlier times. Spells that would pass through the millenniums, down through the centuries. Every witch's book or Grimoire, contains these spells in some form or another. Some Grimoires hold special secrets, links to those ancient times and the priest in Uruk. Kat's book was one of those.

Matthew Hopkins knew nothing of this but he did know the book contained the names of all the witches of England. It was the reason he had been sent, as a

Traveller, with the task of destroying every witch that lived. He never questioned why, The voice in his head, he was certain, was that of God and it was telling him the first witch was the Devil, who appeared as a serpent to the first man and woman on earth, casting a spell upon them.

Hopkins had already found reference in the Grimoire to witch hunts of early times and how the witches could cast spells to cloak themselves and deflect the witch-hunter's interest in them. He was already familiar with the recent witch hunts in Germany, having been there himself. He had read of the trials of the Pendle witches in Lancashire in 1612, one of the most famous in English history.

He knew well of the writings of King James 1 and his book Daemonologie on how to denounce and prosecute the practitioners of witchcraft. Hopkins had built his reputation as a witch hunter on it. Now all he had to do was unlock the secrets within the book, find the names of the witches and where they resided. He turned the pages but all he saw was spells and incantations, instructions for young witches, health and healing spells, chants to protect against evil spirits.

Hopkins was standing in the witches' cottage and he turned to Jac beside him.

"Bring the witch, Mary Clowes to me. She will know how to unlock the book."

Jac stepped outside to where the old woman was held, manacled and chained to a wagon. She was released by one of Hopkins' men and Jac pushed her roughly into the cottage. Hopkins handed the book to her. She began to tremble as she held it.

"You should not be in possession of this book," she

quivered, "it is a witch's book, for her only. It will possess you, witchfinder, and you will be doomed."

"Unlock the book, crone, or you will endure torture and pain you would not believe possible." Jac spat out the words.

"I cannot, it is not my book. I am but a simple healer and maker of herbal remedies. This is a book of high order. It must not be tampered with."

"Open the book's list of witches, old woman, or you will not live to see another day." Hopkins began to draw his sword but Jac stopped him as she turned to the woman, revealing 'pricking' needles in her hand.

"Remember this? Remember the pain?" She said, "You confessed to being a witch and you will be hanged for sure if you do not help the witchfinder."

Mary Clowes waved a hand over the cover of the book and chanted:

"bring upon The Power of Three,

the names of witches let me see."

The pentangle on the book's cover began to spin and Hopkins wrested it from the witch. He turned the pages and the names seemed to appear in a flurry, but he could not read them.

"What trickery is this? Tell me the names." He handed the book back to Mary. She gave him first her own name, then John Lowes, the vicar, Anne Alderman, Rebecca Morris and Mary Bacon of Chattisham. Sarah Spindler, Ian Linstead, Thomas Everard and his wife Mary of Halesworth. Then she named Anne Leech and Anne Wright. Now, Mary told him, he would not only have names of witches of the present day. The book also told of past and future trials, of people accused of witchcraft in Salem, colonial Massachusetts in 1692. He felt as if the book itself was talking to him, inside his head. This was indeed witchcraft, first hand, and he began to savour and relish all it was revealing.

Hopkins had seized paper and a quill. The names in his head appeared as fast as he could write them down. Bridget Bishop, Sarah Good, Rebecca Nurse, Susannah Martin, Elisabeth Howe and Sarah Wildes. The more names Hopkins wrote down, the more the book was drawing him in. He was a Traveller. He knew, with the help of his Time Masters, he could Travel forward to manifest himself as the witch hunter in future trials, not as Matthew Hopkins but as anyone given to God's work to find and condemn witches. This was truly the Devil's own book and he spread word it was in his possession. He would be the greatest witch hunter of all Time.

23
ACCUSED AND CONDEMNED

Gabriel said what we were doing was dangerous but we had to retrieve Kat's Grimoire. She was agitated. She kept hearing from the book. It was telling her Mary Clowes, a witch of Yoxford, was threatened with torture and death by Matthew Hopkins if she did not unlock the book's secrets and reveal the names of all witches. Mary cast a spell, calling upon the Power of Three, like an exorcism, not on the book but on Hopkins himself. The Grimoire had assisted her, revealing certain names we learned, easily convincing the Witchfinder he really possessed the Devil's own book.

We had stopped overnight at The White Hart in Witham, an Essex town of wool merchants in the Witchfinder's own county. But after a meal and sleep we had left, without incident, very early in the morning and rode for Brandeston to see if we could find Tom Cobbold to help us. I kept looking back as we rode because I had an uneasy feeling someone was still following us

Here then, we skirted the edge of Brandeston and arrived safely at the Crossed Swords where we found Tom who said he had enlisted help from others to join and support us if we were to fight the Witchfinder again. Madeleine set out some food on a table, a simple fare of a salat followed by mutton pie, turnip and skirret with a tankard of ale each to wash it down. She said she would keep watch for Hopkins' men as we began to eat heartily.

There was a commotion coming from the entrance to the inn. My heart leaped, thinking this was it, Hopkins had discovered we were here. Then I caught sight of several Royalist soldiers. Leading them was Captain Dagger. I knew now we had been followed, all the way from London and I had a very bad feeling about it. He was waving pistols around, much to the protestations of Madeleine.

"I know they are here. They are under arrest for desertion and horse theft." He was shouting. I reached for a pistol but realised I had, stupidly, left mine in a saddle bag. I went for my sword instead but Gubbins was ahead of me, two pistols in hand. Never bring only swords to a pistol party I remembered.

The soldiers, seeing us, had charged into the dining room. In a fraction of a second we had upturned the oak table, the remains of the food flying everywhere, as we used it as a shield against the pistols fired at us. Gubbins returned fire and dropped two of the men. I don't know what made me think of it but I was sure Captain Dagger would not be killed because I would come against him again in the future, in 1646. How could that be? I was fencing him and he was good. Sword play at such speed I thought I was fighting a daemon. Kat was beside me, fighting another Royalist, winning by the look of it. Gubbins was holding two men at bay. It was then I sensed something I had not felt since I fought the Time Violator at Hampton Court in 1646.

"Hold." I shouted. "Why are you doing this? You have been sent haven't you? You're a Traveller, the

Time Masters have sent you to stop us reaching the Witchfinder General. They want the book, don't they?"

"How perceptive of you, witch. We know who you are. You cannot win." Dagger grinned as he came for me again. Steel on steel, our swords clashed.

"Only you can't win." I shouted. "Your time in this year is up." I knew I could do it. Summon the Time Power. I froze everyone else in the room. I have the power to do that with Time Violators and Travellers. I am a Time Princess. I opened up the floor with a cavernous crack from wall to wall. Captain Dagger was astride the gap as it widened. He reached for the help of another man but they were rigid, rooted to the spot, although aware of what was happening to them.

The crack grew wider as the flames began to lick and heat emerged from the depths. I was sending Captain Dagger and his men to Oblivion. For now, their fight was over. Perhaps history had changed and I would never meet him again. I did not feel bad about it. As a Traveller he might have another life but for now he would cause us no more harm.

The flames rose, the crack widened and one by one the Royalists disappeared with their captain, a look of incomprehension and horror on their faces. I sealed the cracks and we righted the tables.

"Wow!" Exclaimed Kat. "How did you do that?"

"Time Power." I said

Gubbins smiled at me. He'd seen it all before.

***

"A clever trick and much as you would expect of witches."

Matthew Hopkins was behind us and as the floor sealed Jac appeared in front with several Roundheads.

"Not again." I sighed, looking at Kat. I summoned all my power and directed it at Hopkins but he just stood and laughed at me, a cruel laugh.

"Do you think your witch's power will work on the Witchfinder General, the greatest witch hunter of all time? Seize them."

It was true, my Time Power was not working on him or his men. Jac though began to waver a little. She had seen before what I could do. But it was too late. Jac had fired her pistol straight at Gabriel and he sank to his knees, clutching his chest with a bloodied hand, just above his heart.

"I told you I would get your boyfriend." She crowed. The soldiers had their pistols aimed at us and we realised we had no choice but to put down our weapons. It was then I noticed Tom Cobbold had disappeared. He has a habit of doing that.

We were taken outside the inn and once again marched through the village to the witches' cottage. There were several carts, each with women manacled and held in chains. Mary of Yoxford was one of them, the others I did not recognise. There was no sign of Anne Leech or Anne Wright but John Lowes, the vicar was there. We were made to change out of our men's clothes and put on those belonging to the witches, then Kat and I were pushed roughly into a cart and bound in the same way, the metal handcuffs biting into our wrists.

The Witchfinder's troop joined up and we set out in convoy, as the villagers came out of their houses to jeer and throw rotten eggs and vegetables at us.

The journey to Bury St. Edmunds, for that was where they were taking us, was arduous, bound as we were by the manacles and chains. We arrived in the town to be met by crowds who seemed to know of the arrival of eighteen witches accused of acts of maleficium and sorcery. Like the villages before them they threw rotten food, fish, eggs and the contents of chamber pots at us, shouting: 'witches will die'. We had been made to stand as the carts rumbled through the streets, swaying with their motion. We caught sight as we passed a courtyard of a gibbet, a gallows, prepared for hangings.

We came at last to a forbidding building that housed the gaol, where we were marched down steps and all thrown into one big dungeon cell, a steel cage from which there was no escape. The barred door was slammed. The stench was unbearable and women began to moan and wail. The vicar was doing his best to placate everyone but to no avail.

Kat stared at me in the half-light.

"What are we to do, Klaudia? This cannot be happening to us. I want to go home. Please."

What could I do? My Time Power had not worked on Hopkins. We were told we would be brought before the justices in the morning and that every case against us was a foregone conclusion as we had all confessed to witchcraft. We being charged as Anne Leech and Anne Wright. Matthew Hopkins had gathered and presented all the evidence and sought assistance of the many people supposedly involved in bringing us to trial.

Doctors, lawyers, constables, the justices themselves. We sat waiting. Some revolting gruel was pushed into the cell by a gaoler but no one dared eat any of it.

The half-light turned to dark and I suppose we must have slept for a while because I woke to a thin stream of sunlight, a symbol of a moment of hope piercing the darkness of the dungeon.

One by one we were led, with rattling chains, our clothes stinking and our hair matted with the filth of the previous day and a night in gaol. We climbed stairs and entered the dock of a court room. The Justices of the Assizes were assembled, led by John Godbolt and presided over as well by two Suffolk clergymen, Samuel Fairclough and Edmund Callamy. The court was filled with onlookers, come to see the accused witches be condemned.

My heart sank as Matthew Hopkins appeared, holding Kat's Grimoire. John Stearne and Jac were beside him.

"By special commission granted by the Oyer and Terminer, this court is in session." Rang out the words.

"The first of the accused," Hopkins announced, "be John Lowes, Vicar of Brandeston. He confessed to a teat beneath his tongue, on which he suckles his Imps. Tell us, vicar, of your sinking of a ship and other crimes, all of what you told us in your confession." The vicar looked crestfallen but he answered.

"One of my Imps swam to a ship," he began, "sailing by the mouth of the Stour. The ship began travelling up and down, as if water had been boiled in a pot. It sank, making fourteen widows in one quarter of an hour."

"Did you not grieve to see so many people die?" Hopkins asked.

"No, I was joyful to see what power my Imps had."
Hopkins turned to a woman beside us in the dock.
"And you, your name?" He questioned
"Anna." Was all she would say.
"Well, Anna, tell us what you told the Witchfinder General in your confession," came from the Justice.
"The devil came to me as a shaggy red dog and tempted me to kill my children. Then he came to me as a black bee. He told me not to eat or drink in prison, that I may starve to death rather than give you satisfaction. He gave me a knife to kill myself but I will not leave my familiars or my Imps." Then the Witchfinder General looked at Kat and me. He turned to the bench, pretending to read from Kat's Grimoire.

"These two, Lord Justice, may it please you, confessed to worse. Their names are Anne Leech and Anne Wright. Between them they killed pigs they were displeased with and this one killed her husband," he said, pointing at me.

"They look not old enough to have husbands." Said one of the clergymen and the court laughed.

"That is their witches' deception. They stand before you as young girls. Condemn them and on the morrow as they hang you will see they are hags and old practitioners of witchcraft and magik. You will see this manifested."

"We will take your word on this, Master Hopkins, and if what you say is true they will be hanged by the neck, the life choked slowly out of them, until they are dead. May the Lord have mercy upon them."

That was it. I could not believe this was happening. We were not allowed to say a word and we, with the others, were led at the end of the day back to the gaol cell. I held Kat's hand and felt she was holding back the tears. I tried to summon my Time Power to get us out of there. Nothing. I called to Gubbins but I did not know what had happened to him when we were taken from Brandeston. I thought he must be dead because there was no answer.

We sat in the putrid, filthy stench of the dungeon. Frightened. Eighteen of us accused and condemned to die the following day, the 27th August 1645. This was unfair, unjust, it was all a fake. Hopkins, Stearne, Jac, how could the Justices believe them? But Hopkins had prepared the evidence, the confessions, like a lawyer, and held us as if we really were Anne Leech and Anne Wright. I was not so worried about myself. I am a Traveller and I might have another life. But what about Kat? I wanted to cry myself for what had happened to her, my friend. It was my fault. I should have stopped her trying to put a spell on Jac. There was no help from the Lords Temporal.

I thought about the real Anne Leech and Anne Wright. What had happened to them? They had disappeared off the face of the earth. And what of Tom Cobbold and his sister Madeleine? Had they really been part of a plot to have us captured and condemned? They could appear and disappear at will. Here we were, about to die.

It was morning again and there were voices in my head. Was it the Lords Temporal at last? I thought of something.

"Do you still have the potion the witches gave us?" I whispered to Kat.

"Yes, do you?"

"Right here."

"What good will it do?"

"I don't know, but I'm willing to give it a try. When they come for us, sprinkle it around. It might work."

"What if it doesn't?"

I had no answer to that.

There was a rattle of keys and the gaoler, with several soldiers, came down the steps. He unlocked the door and motioned us out and up the steps. He crossed himself as he did so.

We stepped into bright August sunlight to find ourselves in a courtyard and marched to the gallows, ropes hanging down in ominous preparation. A big crowd had gathered.

John Lowes, the Vicar of Brandeston, insisted on conducting his own funeral service, even though he held up a charm, a bewitched charm he claimed would prevent him from being hanged. But he was led to the gallows and we watched in horror as the rope was slipped around his head. Three women were led up beside him, wailing softly.

I was not going to stand for this. I took out the flask of witches' potion and Kat did the same. We sprinkled it all around us as soldiers came to lead us to the gallows.

I could not believe what happened. It was as if time stood still. Everyone around us appeared to be frozen, captive by the potion's spell. Matthew Hopkins stood like a Tussaud waxwork, John Stearne and Jac the same beside him. Hopkins had Kat's Grimoire in his hand and what was strange was the pentangle on the cover was spinning, the only movement in the whole courtyard. There was an eerie silence.

Thinking my eyes were deceiving me, Anne Leech

and Anne Wright appeared as if from nowhere. With them, and I could not believe it, were Gabriel Gubbins, my Gabriel, he was alive, and Tom Cobbold with him. The two Annes looked just like us, like twins, and they took our place at the hands of the soldiers.

We moved towards the shadows as people began to come out of the trance-like state. Angry, I started to walk towards Jac and the Witchfinder General but Gubbins held me back.

"Hold, Somerset, it is not yet time. The Voices tell me we cannot stop this now. It is written in time but Tom has delivered to the Judges of the Assizes the letter we brought from Parliament. Hopkins' day will be over."

We had to turn away as, one by one, eighteen accused of witchcraft were hanged and there was nothing we could do. The horror of it all was made worse as Anne Leech and Anne Wright were led to their deaths. They no longer looked like me and Kat. They had become old hags, looking like you imagine witches to look. Then something really strange happened.

Hopkins turned a page in the Grimoire and there, staring at him, was an Imp. He drew back as he watched in horror the shape appearing before him. The Imp's face contorted as it transfigured and became INPA, the Mesopotamian god of fever. Matthew Hopkins had no time to pull away, indeed the Grimoire would not leave his grip, it was holding him, rigid, as the Imp god sneezed and coughed.

Hopkins saw a haze before him. It too changed shape, like a murmuration of starlings and their acrobatic mass, swirling before his eyes. The haze twisted, turned and disappeared through the witchfinder's nostrils, filling his chest and his body with an aching, feverish sensation.

At last the book released him and he threw it down as he began to cough and sneeze. Some liquid trickled from the corners of his mouth and he cursed as he wiped it away with the white sleeve of his shirt. The sleeve was covered with his own mucous and blood. He stumbled and fell backwards, sensing he was the victim of something far beyond the powers of the Witchfinder General.

He groaned as he coughed more blood. The Grimoire lay at his feet, the pentangle on its cover spinning wildly, as if the book was triumphant. Jac picked it up and slipped into the watching crowd, mingling with the people of Bury St. Edmunds, come to see a good hanging. We quickly followed her but she had disappeared in the pressing throng.

"Come, we have horses ready, we must leave." Said Gabriel.

"But my book." Kat pressed.

"I am sure Jac will follow us if we show ourselves to be leaving. She will do everything to stop you returning home." Tom Cobbold said, "let her follow us and then we can seize the book."

We agreed to this and found ourselves on the way back to Brandeston. When I asked why, you could have knocked me over with a Royalist feather. Tom Cobbold told us he was not only a Traveller but that he had been my Caller. Although Gubbins had 'Called' me to 1647, it was Tom who had brought me to the church at Brandeston in 1645, to save Kat and the Grimoire. By going back to the church we had a way home.

So we arrived at All Saints church, where I had first

met the poor vicar. Gabriel said he would have liked us to go to Oxford but it would take days and it was better we should Travel from here. He was sure the Voices had told him so. I sensed this as well, from the Lords Temporal.

Here we were again, in Brandeston, and it was no surprise to find Jac waiting for us, on the steps of the church, with a troop of Hopkins' soldiers, though the Witchfinder was nowhere in sight. I cast a glance to Kat and Gabriel.

"She's mine." I said to the others. No one protested. I engaged swords with Jac. I fought her up the steps and pushed her with parry and lunge, back into the church, soldiers beside her fighting Kat, Gabriel and Tom Cobbold. We were like the Three Musketeers and d'artagnan, together on the good side of Time.

I caught Jac off guard for a fraction of a moment and her face contorted. I saw the weird, devil-like mask she had been wearing at our Halloween party. Her body was changing and she was becoming that Roundhead again, the one in my nightmare. Now I knew whatever it was it had Jac in its power. There was only one thing for it. Power versus Power. I felt a fit coming on, all my pent up ADHD being released. This was not anger but cold and calculating action to destroy a Time Violator once again. I could not think of it as Jac and I could not help her. Perhaps I would feel guilty the rest of my life but there was only one thing to do.

There was a stained glass window at the end of the church, above the altar. It depicted mediaeval interpretations of the bible, saints, God and the angels. They began to move, come to life before our eyes. The fighting stopped. The soldiers stood with their mouths open as they stared at the sight of Jac, or at least, the manifestation of Jac, rising into the air and floating backwards towards the image of a griffon with its clawed foot holding down a serpent.

Just at this point I hooked the Grimoire out of Jac's hand with the tip of my sword and tossed it to Kat's waiting catch. Jac flew backwards into the window and as all the images stopped moving her own image became a winged devil frozen in the stained glass. I had sent her to Oblivion.

The soldiers threw down their swords and ran out of the church. We walked over to the font and at this moment Madeleine appeared from the secret passage to the inn.

"It was Tom and Madeleine who were sent as Travellers to help you." Said Gabriel

"And the two Annes, they were true witches and Travellers also." Said Tom.

"But they died, hanged as witches." I protested.

"True, but they will live again, if they have more lives left to them. Sometimes sacrifices have to be made. They volunteered. Theirs was to save you and the Grimoire. The Justices and Parliament will question the Witchfinder's actions. It may take time but be sure Matthew Hopkins' day will be over."

"The Grimoire knows," Kat said, "Mary of Yoxford's spell was an exorcism of the devil in Hopkins. He will not live long, it tells me."

"Then we are done here, let us all away. Go home, Somerset and Kat. Take the book and guard it with your lives. We will meet again, Klaudia, we have unfinished business in 1647." Gabriel said, looking more handsome than ever. Suddenly I didn't want to leave him. I had feelings I could not explain but I was sure that I would die if I never saw him again.

"Are you an angel, Gabriel?" I asked. He smiled at this as we put our hands on the rim of the font and the familiar tingling sensation began.

"Some may say so," he laughed, as he disappeared like a clearing mist on the water.

"Thank you Tom, Madeleine." I said to them. I really did have my doubts about you but I can see now how it all had to work. What will you do? Will you Travel?"

"Who knows? Perhaps back to sea, perhaps to another time and place. For now though, we will continue our campaign against the Witchfinder General. Perhaps you will read of us in your history books."

Kat and I both laughed at this, as Time took control and we were gone from Brandeston. Forever.

EPILOGUE

It was Scary Mary who broke the silence.

"The power of the Time Masters was so great we knew we and the Lords Temporal had a real fight on our hands when Kat disappeared."

"It was the only reason I agreed to let you go, Klaudia." Mum said, as she hugged me tightly to her. I did not resist. It was comforting to know so many people had been rooting for us in our battle against the Witchfinder General, Jac and the evil side of Time itself.

Kat and I had found ourselves back at the Halloween party *before* Kat had taken a mirror out of her satchel, with the small bag containing the onyx. She had placed the picture of Jac on the mugwort, about to chant the spell. I placed a hand on hers.

"No Kat, not that way, no banishing spell. You need to learn a lot more about your Grimoire before you're ready." She agreed with me but not really knowing why. She remembered something of what actually happened but she was confused because we were back just before it all began. I walked over to Jac.

"No one invited you, Jac. No one likes you. In fact, everyone hates you. You're a bully and a coward. You know what happened. I know what happened. Kat does not remember much. You're really lucky to be here. If it was not for the Lords Temporal granting clemency you would still be part of a stained glass window in 1645.

I'm not going to fight you, because I know I will win. You know I will win, don't you, Jac?"

Typical Jac. She stuck out her tongue, pierced with its ring. It seemed to have a life of its own, her tongue. Jac and her mates turned and left the party. It was then Scary Mary and mum came over and Mary said her piece.

We four, me, Kat, Bran and Slick Alice escaped the main party for the Tapestry Room and as I told the others all that Kat and I had been through, we Googled Matthew Hopkins.

He was called to account by Parliament and the Judges of the Assizes. He still claimed he had the Devil's book to guide him in his witch hunting. He published a paper of his own: 'In answer to severall QUERIES LATELY,' delivered to the Judges for the County of Norfolk and 'for the benefit of the whole KINGDOM.' Defending his actions he asked and answered his own questions:

'Q. That he must needs be the greatest witch, sorcerer and wizard himself, else he could not do it.'

'A. If satan's kingdom be divided against itself, how shall it stand?'

'Q. If he never went so far as is` before mentioned, yet for certain he met with the Devil, and cheated him of his booke, wherein were written all the witches' names in England; and if he looks on any witch he can tell, by her countenance what she is; so by this his help is from the Devil.'

Now you and I know otherwise because you have read the whole story. Well almost. Matthew Hopkins,

Witchfinder General, did have as many as three hundred 'witches' condemned and hanged before he was brought to account, through the publishing of a certain newspaper, the Moderate Intelligencer by John Dillingham and Robert White. The Reverend John Gaule campaigned Valentine Walton, Parliament and the people against the Witchfinder.

After the party I had a text from Gabriel Gubbins saying, 'TIME TO TRAVEL.' I was to keep my promise and help him find King Charles 1 who had disappeared in 1647.

It was the year Matthew Hopkins, Witchfinder General, died of a nasty disease that makes you sneeze and cough up blood. He was buried in a graveyard of the Church of St. Mary at Mistley Heath.

Or so the legends say.

Klaudia Cay.